LUNA STATION
QUARTERLY

Issue 041 | March 2020

Editor-in-Chief
Jennifer Lyn Parsons

Editors
Rocky Breen • Linda Codega • Angelica Fyfe
Shel Graves • Cathrin Hagey • Sarah McGill
Cait Ryan • Carly Racklin • Shanna Ross
Tamara Lee Rutledge • Gô Shoemake • Margaret Stewart

LUNA STATION PRESS
NEW JERSEY

First Paperback Edition March 2020
ISBN: 978-1-949077-11-7

Luna Station Quarterly publishes short fiction on March 1st, June 1st,
September 1st, and December 1st. For more information and submission
guidelines, please visit our website at lunastationquarterly.com

For Luna Station Press

Creative Director - Tara Quinn Lindsey
Editor-in-Chief & Founder - Jennifer Lyn Parsons

 LUNA STATION PRESS

www.lunastationpress.com

CONTENTS

Editorial

Jennifer Lyn Parsons

Jennifer Lyn Parsons is a writer, programmer, and maker. With influences ranging from Laura Ingalls Wilder to Jim Jarmusch, her tales feature a rare physicality with details that feel hand-carved. When not writing code or prose, she is also the editor-in-chief of the venerable Luna Station Quarterly. She finds joy in video games, comics books, discovering music new and old, and making things out of wool, paper, and wood.

There are two sides to Luna Station Quarterly. One does not function without the other, they're forever intertwined. The first is you, the reader. Without you there would be no purpose for the magazine you now read. These pages, these stories, there is no need for them without you to enjoy them or, at the least, take from them what you will.

Our readers are a community. We see you on social media, we note your presence on Patreon and our website and whenever you make a purchase of an issue or anthology. In all these ways, you show us how much you care about and support LSQ and the work it does to support women-identified authors. In a world that grows darker by the day, those small connections mean everything.

Then there are those times that you reach out and tell us directly what a story has meant to you. Well, those times are truly special. We love to hear from you! It gives us a boost of inspiration in this work we do and helps us to remember what a brighter future might look like, or what dark future may come to fruition if we're not careful, or yes, even what a world long ago or far away has to show us about being human.

The other half of this helix, twisting like DNA through the

strands of story, is our staff and authors. Together we create this thing, build it and give it life. From the day-to-day of running and writing the blog, to the time taken to read every submission that comes through our inbox, our staff works to ensure that the women-identified folks around the world have a voice in genre fiction. We, too, are a community. We support each other and share the load of what it means to be a writer of the fantastique in a world bent on making us believe that imagination and story have no purpose anymore.

That structure allows us the freedom and strength to hold the door open for new and emerging voices. We bring them into the fold, welcoming them as best we can around a campfire fueled by a passion for story. In almost every issue we have a new author, someone the world has never read before, have a chance to share their tale with the world. And such stories they are! While it is said that all the stories have already been written, our authors consistently surprise us with the infinite variations still out there, undiscovered.

In addition to our story authors and the quarterly, those wonderful folks who write for our blog bring new thoughts and ideas into the light every day of the week. They introduce us to stories we have been curious about, give us new ideas to ponder, and remind us of the breadth of thought that's possible when all of humanity gets to share its voice.

All of us together form the whole of what LSQ is about, why we are here and what we have to offer the world. So, to our readers and our writers, to our staff and to our supporters, welcome to the eleventh year of Luna Station Quarterly. Let us be the warp and the weft of countless worlds both real and imagined. May the two halves of our community continue to weave together the shared story of our worlds.

L S Q | 041

Salt

Rosemary Melchior

Rosemary Melchior lives in New York City, where she works in advertising. Her writing has appeared in countless pitch decks, in Writer's Digest as a contest winner, and here in LSQ. An avid traveler, she has a talent for finding the perfect breakfast spot no matter where she is.

Salt air slaps her face as she steps off the wooden ship, as if the island is already offended at her presence there. Pulling her fur cloak tighter around her shoulders, Sigga lifts her chin against the wind and continues down the gangplank.

There are not many there to meet them— an older official, his face ruddy under his navy cap, and a small scattering of young men and women to see who's turned up on the ship this time. Who's been newly given over to this barren island of criminals.

"Welcome!" the official shouts, as if any of them had a choice in coming. His fingers rest on a rusted knife hanging from his belt.

A woman with a bruised cheek raises her hand to return the greeting, the civility of society not yet beaten out of her by the waves. Sigga heard that the woman was a thief, though she doesn't look like much of anything now. On the prisoner ship over from her homeland to this rock bared from the ocean, Sigga kept to herself. At sixteen she wasn't the youngest passenger. Her crimes were not as dangerous as the others'— murder, whoring, assault, and thievery— but the word they branded her at the docks made the others wary of her. *Witch.*

No matter how they make their money, everyone knows to stay away from witches.

Finally, her feet touch the ground with a thump. The land is frozen solid, the small clumps of dirt as hard as stones. Scuffing the toes of her boot through brittle grass, she reminds herself that she knew this is how it would be. Still, the sensation is strange after so many days on the water.

The official scans their faces as the last person departs the ship. Satisfied, he takes a few steps forward. "Now that you're here, there are few options open to you. You can join us at our settlement and follow our rules. Give whatever supplies you have to the keeper of the storehouse and we'll give you a role here. We share all of our resources and we'll help you stay alive for as long as we're able."

Sigga's companions exchange glances and murmurs, but she keeps her mouth locked tight. She's not going to join some village run by a man, not after what happened last time. After what they did to her.

As he continues, the official's voice darkens and he leans towards them. "If you're thinking that you're fresh and strong, that you can come in here and take what you wish, know that you are wrong. We will tear your flesh from the bone and use your body to survive the winter."

A shiver runs down Sigga's spine, but she refuses to let it show.

The official watches his words sink in, a wicked smile curling across his face. "If that doesn't work for you, you can try your luck further inland or at the cliffs. Know that there's more danger out there than there is in here— people who choose to live alone on this island can't be trusted." He pauses. "They tend to go a little mad."

With that, his welcome speech is completed. He turns around

on his heel, knife flashing in the sunlight, and heads back to the cluster of thatched huts that make up the settlement on this isolated island. Everyone else hurries to join him; Sigga watches them go. It's probably their best chance for survival.

Alone, she scans the horizon and the hills before she makes her decision. To the north. The settlement is circled by a crude wooden fence, and Sigga will have to go around it to get to where she wants. Tucking her hands against her ribs to keep them warm, she leaves the shore behind her.

The island has no name, or that isn't correct— the island has too many names to be known by just one. *Prisoner's Rock. Isle of Exiles. Land of Ice and Stone. Dragon Back.* Sigga has read about it under all of its names.

A place where people get sent to be forgotten.

***

Exertion makes her face hot, even as her nose freezes. The settlement is far behind her now and the ship disappeared into the horizon, but she's planned for this. Sigga has everything she needs, tucked beneath her clothes and in the small woolen bag that they allowed her. She's heading north, as far north as she can go.

"Ho there!" The voice comes sudden from the hills, and she glances up to find a boy her age standing on the greening moss. He's from the island, his black hair long and shaggy around his chin. When she doesn't stop, he lopes down the hill to catch her.

"You!" he says again when he reaches her. "You're new. You'll want to turn around now. If you go out there, you'll die."

She doesn't bother slowing her pace; she has to cover as much ground as she can before night falls. "Isn't that the point of this island?"

He lets out a sigh, but the corner of his mouth turns up. "If you go out there, you'll die *quicker*."

Checking the sun to make sure she's still headed due north, her boot heels knife against the harsh ground. "Perhaps. Perhaps not."

He runs a hand through his tangled hair, keeping even with her. "There's always someone on every boat who thinks they can survive on their own."

"And you come to look out for them?" She shouldn't be interacting with him, but there's a gleam in his brown eyes that pulls her focus. "How charitable."

Now he laughs outright. "Who are you and why were you sent here?"

"Sigga," she tells him. As for the rest? Anger no longer burns in her chest to keep her warm; over the days spent in her village's dirty jail and the bowels of the ship, it compressed, like snow tamped down into a frozen ball of ice. She carries it now like a weapon. "I'm here for the same reason that everyone else is. I made the wrong man angry."

Pleased with her answer, the boy introduces himself with a short bow. "I'm Hem."

Her foot falters, skittering over black rock. "Like the saga."

"Yes. Like Hem and his axe of light." The boy smiles ruefully, peeking over at her from underneath long lashes. "Except he never stabbed anyone."

She knows all of the sagas. After, they said she'd read too many forbidden tales, but she didn't— she'd read adventurer's journals, the bound letters of men and women who came before her, and the sagas in every interpretation. This doesn't scare her.

Raising an eyebrow, she responds to the boy. "That's a story I'll have to hear."

His face brightens in the afternoon sun, and she wonders how long he's been trapped here. "Are you planning to come back then?"

"Yes." This is one thing she's certain about. This island will not kill her.

"Then I'll wait for you," he promises. Pausing for a moment, he rushes out the remaining words. "Stay away from the valley— it seems like a good place to avoid the wind, but there are dangerous men who keep their camp there."

"Thank you," she says, and she means it. He stops walking with her after that, but she feels him watching her back until the distance takes even that away.

***

When night comes, the temperature drops like a stone tossed in a well.

Remembering the survival stories that she's read, she huddles behind a mound of land and stacks rocks to block out the wind. She curls up, pulling her cloak tight around her body. Boots stuffed with rabbit fur, her toes are the only part of her that aren't cold. Her feet sweated on the boat, but it was all worth it for this small bit of warmth.

Laying down, her mind doesn't quiet. There is a low circle of moonlight above her, and she thinks of the stories that brought her here. Not the good ones, but the others.

How easy it was for a man to whisper about seeing her in that same moonlight, dressed in nothing but her long brown hair. That those books she'd read were full of evil lies of dragons and sprites and blood. Or how she was spotted comforting a crying friend and stealing the tears off of her face for later. (How would she save them? For what? Such nonsense.) The word *'witch'* built around them like a fire being stoked. More powerful, more believed, with every uttering.

He took her away from her friends, ruined her reputation with the village, caused her own family to cast her out of home when they started to believe the stories—all to protect the small powers that he had gathered while leading the village. How fragile his pride.

Forcing her eyes closed, Sigga tells herself to sleep. Her hands curl tightly against her stomach for warmth, but the thoughts won't quiet, not when she's so close.

It started so simply, before. The leader of the village decided to build the new village road right by the inn he owned, even though the route didn't make sense. He issued a new tax against those with more than five horses, so high that soon no one had more horses than him, just the same. He pardoned his friends and found accusations against their enemies. His purse grew with coin that never should have belonged to him. No one else could see it, until she started to tell them.

It was exactly as she said to Hem: Her words made the wrong man angry, and now here she is.

***

The next morning dawns still and clear, the sky unbearably blue above her. As directed by the sun, she keeps walking north across the endless land.

Green lichen is frozen underfoot, crackling like a fist with every step. When she's been walking for a few hours, she tugs at the sun-warmed moss and places it in her bag for later, insulation when she sleeps. The nights won't get any kinder, she knows; the journals she's read say it only gets worse.

Wind sears her like hellfire as the landscape opens up. A black rock tower rises in the distance, its cap ringed in fog, but her steps don't seem to take her any closer. Her fingers freeze despite their wraps; her ears burn underneath her cloak's furred hood. She doesn't dare dig into the store of food she hoarded and hid during the ship ride over yet, and her stomach howls with the wind.

It's early afternoon when she comes to the valley that Hem mentioned, a thread carved out of the land and walled in black rocks. There's a hint of a river at the bottom and her body is so tempted to climb down, to walk without the scream of the wind in her ears.

Hem's words echo in her mind. There are wild men down there. It's hard to make herself bow her head against the wind and leave it behind, but she does it. She'll need to be on alert for those who camp there. No weapons are allowed on the ship, no knives tucked down tunics or sewn into hems. She has nothing but her wits and the rocks around her to defend herself, and her wits haven't served her so well lately.

Sigga gives the valley a wide berth, adding unknown time to her journey. As she walks, a far-off screech makes her heart stop. The men? An animal?

Her own foolish pulse?

Harsh air stings her lungs as her breath comes quicker. Another sound follows her, a dark laugh torn from an angry throat. She's not imagining it; those men are coming.

Running now, she crests a low hill and pauses. A wide river cuts in from the surrounding sea, both ends invisible in the distance. Ice glazes the surface but she can't tell how thick it is. If it will hold her. There's no other way for her to go.

Sliding down to the river's edge, she sets her boot on the ice. A crack echoes from nearby and she makes a decision: cold is better than wet. She goes to her knees, then lower to spread out her weight, and pushes herself across the surface of the river. Ice crystals snag against her skin.

The river groans around her, hungry and alive. She hears it when something joins her on the ice, but she keeps her eyes forward. A numbness sneaks past her dress despite the layers. When she reaches the far side, she digs her fingernails into the dirt to scramble up the bank. There's a flash of black behind her but she doesn't turn around to see them; she keeps running north.

If she was looking for hospitable land, she would have turned back long ago. Would have crawled back to the settlement and begged them to take her in.

But she isn't. She's looking for something more.

***

The next morning, the snow comes.

When she wakes, a light dusting covers the ground and she can see animal markings around the remains of her campfire. Rabbits or fox? It's too blurred for her to tell how dangerous.

Her fingers crack like sticks when she forces her grip tighter around her bag. Nothing she can do but continue, she tells herself, although the words don't feel as strong as they did before.

Leaving her camp behind, Sigga continues north. Her mother would tell her to wrap her sore feet with linens, to staunch the blood before it wrecks her boots. Half-blinded by the snow and her own sour thoughts, Sigga doesn't see the rock until she stumbles over it.

Flat on the ground, she tips her chin to glare and blanches at what she sees. It's not a rock that she's tripped over, but a body frozen in ice, half-buried under stones and peat. The body's arm is clearly broken; they'd never make it further like that. Its face is a handbreadth from hers. *Close like...*

In a moment, she's *here* and also *there*, on her last free day in the village. When her family turned her out, the villagers came for her, massing in the streets like a flood. They knew she was nothing. Alone.

She fled to the only place she knew they wouldn't go, the small dark space carved out beneath the village cold house. It was some time before her eyes adjusted to the blackness, before she realized what was next to her. A body, dead only a few days. She hadn't known. They would keep it until spring thawed the ground for burial; maybe Sigga's body would join it. No, she knew better, witches didn't get buried, they got burned. Or hung or *cleansed*, lungs full of lake water. Cheek pressed against the packed dirt floor, she listened to the mob outside calling for her neck while staring into the corpse's open eyes.

The shivers she had then flood her body now.

No other way to save herself, she couldn't leave, couldn't move until she wanted to die too, until perhaps she did. All her fear and pain bled into the frozen ground, and that cold climbed up into her instead. When she finally slid away from the corpse, she knew what she wanted to do.

She went out into her village and let them take her away.

Climbing steadily to her feet, she strips this new body of their cloak, whispering prayers all the while. Were they a murderer? A rapist? Did they deserve their death on this island? Does anyone?

That night when she builds the fire, she burns it for hours, until her questions cease to matter. Something has to be worth this.

***

Time loses all sense after that. There are hours where she doesn't think of anything but the white circle of the sun guiding her north and the hard rock of anger in her chest, heavy as her straining heart. Cuts and bruises appear on her skin. Cold burrows into her lungs.

Sigga passes a frozen waterfall, hanging from the gray cliffs like the folds of a dress. She looks at it for too long and she slips, falling on hard ice underneath the cover of snow. Pain spikes up her body. Catching her breath, she brushes away the snow to see the frozen lake underneath her. It's dark and murky in the water, but she sees a round shape bumping up against the crust of ice. Almost like an egg. It's glowing gently beneath the surface. This is a sign.

The northern coast must be close.

Forcing her disjointed body up and into movement, she runs. Air stings her face and she can taste salt again for the first time since she left the coast. She runs until she sees a horizon in the distance, until she's at the gray rocks, a jagged cliff not too high above the ocean. Reaching the edge, she peers over to the water below. There they are.

The ice dragons.

Buried under the icy waves, their tails rip through the water as they swim. Ice crystals crust their eyelids like salt from the ocean when they surface, their heads almost lupine. Their scales gleam blue and green and silver, edged in light and sharp as knives. Wonder and rage dance through her chest.

There are many ways to punish a girl. Sigga let it be known that this frozen island was her biggest fear, whispered like a secret through the village, and a man like that couldn't resist. Arrogant, condescending, he was all of it when he proclaimed her sentence: she was going to Prisoner's Rock. Isle of Exiles. Land of Ice and Stone.

Dragon Back.

Sigga read about the rumors of the dragons, the ones that people didn't believe in. Their breeding ground lies at the northernmost point of an abandoned island. Looking out at the water, a smile breaks over her face for the first time in a while.

He wanted a witch, so she'll give him one. She'll see him burn on the pyre he built for her.

Down in the Kettle Bog, or: Julian and the Frogman

Josie Nuñez

Josie Nuñez is a writer and teacher living in Seattle, Washington. She studied English at Williams College and Medieval Literature at the University of Edinburgh. The main focus of her writing is urban fantasy set in small towns. 'Rural fantasy' doesn't have the same brand recognition, but Josie hopes to change that.

When Amy Wells drops out of the sky on her neat, birch twig broom, she tells me, "We have a frogman problem."

Just like that. She doesn't even take the corncob pipe out of her mouth. How she can fly with that thing dangling from her lips is beyond me.

"Well, aren't you going to get up?" she asks and gnaws the pipe stem.

Doesn't she get splinters?

I'm lying prone on my cloud veranda, a hundred feet over my abandoned apartment. The wind that should be tangling my hair has been skillfully diverted. It took me days of adjustments to get that charm just right. All is still here, and quiet. My back doesn't touch the cloud, because if it did I'd only feel mist. If I don't touch it, if I lie on top of the pearly froth, I can pretend it's soft. I can enjoy the aesthetic, and all my dreams are sweet.

"*Julian*," says Amy, in that particular tone she has. So, I begin to stir. Her toes are dangling over my nose anyway. How long could my doze last with Amy's Doc Martens dripping mud in my face?

She adjusts her shirt cuffs impatiently when she sees me move. "Not speaking yet? Spell still active?"

I nod.

"Well," she grunts, spitting out a mouthful of bruised purple smoke, *"this is all turning out peachy."* Her fingers drum her broomstick, ba-dum, ba-dum.

Amy likes to fuss. I can tell the frogman situation must be more than a rumor this time 'round, because this is more than fussing. I float upward to meet her, close enough to kiss her cheek, so I do. I steal the corncob pipe while I'm at it. Amy's eyes pop, her face a picture of consternation. It's been six months since we've seen each other.

"Of all the bullshit antics," she says. And that's how I know we're still friends.

***

Of course I go with her. An hour later, we've passed out of my dead-end Albany suburb and are soaring in tandem over the Eastern crest of the Berkshires. After half a year spent keeping myself away from loud noises, people, and any activity more exerting than a trip to the 7-11, the rushing air is a slap in the face. It gets worse whenever we rise to avoid a mountain peak. I breathe in sips through a scarf.

The valleys below are dotted with houses and the occasional town, photogenic to the point that it all seems a bit unreal. We are deep in bed-and-breakfast territory here, and the sight of those colonial homes is making Amy even tetchier than she was when she picked me up. She's a farm witch down to her bones. Witchery in the Berkshires is difficult enough without leaf peepers and their cameras.

"It kills me to see them traipsing all over the towns, cooing over how 'relaxing' it is around here while we've been up to our ears in everything from pickling curses to summer howlers! It's been crazy this year!" She has to yell to be heard over the wind. I nod and nod. While some of this is Amy's annual autumn grumbling, the rest is news to me. I should feel guilty for being so behind, but I don't.

"Damn near lost a hand to a howler this past solstice. See!" She waves her right hand at me. We're about twenty feet apart, the minimum recommended distance between flying broomsticks— not so far apart that I can't see the remains of her pinky, gnawed down to the last knuckle. There's that guilt-inducing lack of guilt again, dizzying this time. Oh, Amy. I hadn't even noticed.

I toss her a pot of salve from my backpack. She catches it easily enough, giving me one of her uncertain smiles.

"I'm fine *now*, Hard-hitter," she protests. She keeps the salve, though. It goes into the breast pocket of her tweed coat.

We reach the coven at sunset. Stony Ledge unfolds before us as we descend, like a rumpled, granite tablecloth. The Ledge is an ideal spot in the mountains for witches to gather, with easy broomstick landing and a parking lot nearby. The coven is a blob of practical coats and hats from here. I can just pick out Gabriela by her ever-present khaki duffle bag, no doubt packed with ley line maps and her prized Winchester. She's the first to spot us. She waves us down.

I dip over the top of a beech and let myself float the rest of the way into the clearing. It's strange to me now, walking. I've barely descended for anything other than meals or bathroom breaks in months. Now I wobble along like a sailor freshly returned from sea, trying to keep up with Amy's efficient strides.

"Julian! Merry met," says Marissa, the nearest witch. She breaks off from the chattering huddle to come hug me, and slips me a cider donut as she pulls away. I bob my head in thanks. She adjusts her electric green glasses, blinks at me.

"Oh! Still not, um...?"

No, still not talking. I give her a rueful smile, hoping to convey a sense of, 'Hey, what you gonna do, life's crazy, right?'

"I see." She hands me an extra donut. They're so warm and fresh that I have to cup them in both hands to make sure they don't fall to pieces before I can get them into my mouth. Amy turns around beside me.

"Yes, merry met, merry met, now are we all *here*?" She counts up witches like she counts her prize-winning chickens, her lips moving silently over the numbers.

There are twelve of us now. There used to be thirteen. Amy almost forgets. She flicks her head around, and I notice the way her eyes dull when she catches herself. It's an awkward start to an awkward meeting. Marissa and the twins seem to be the only ones comfortable speaking to me. Our youngest, Sato, was on spring break when I left. I can tell she has questions for me, wants to see how close the gossip hits to the truth. I smile at everyone.

We gather beside a semi-magical and definitely illegal camp-fire, where the Ledge fades into the forest. Claudia lays out the basics: she spotted the frogman in the kettle bog outside of North Adams. Five cats are missing in the area. There are families with newborn babies living on that edge of the town, so we have to act fast. The main issue is numbers. If this frogman is dug in properly, even a full dozen witches will be...challenged in a fight. 'Challenged' is how Claudia phrases it, instead of 'outclassed,' or 'fucked.'

"The last time we did this," she tells us, "that is to say, the last time the Wells Farm coven went up against a fully grown frog-man, was two generations ago." When Amy's grandmother was running the show.

We pass around the "Wells Grimoire and Bestiary" for reference, the battered pages held open to Nana Eugenia Wells' account of the incident. I've only seen a frogman in person once, the frozen corpse of a juvenile. The creature inked onto the page of the Grimoire is easily thrice as big, dwarfing the little witch drawn beside it for reference. Above the illustration, someone has scribbled a skull and crossbones in red ink. I rub it with my thumb. Subtle.

"Eugenia manage to beat it?"

"Barely, working with a group of twenty."

Another round of donuts gets shared out while we absorb this. I realize, suddenly, why they taste so familiar: they're made with cider from Amy's orchard. Under the layer of Marissa's baking charm, I taste apples crushed in a wooden hand-press. I taste the life of a hopeful wasp that got too close, and the muslin Amy used to strain it out. If I concentrated, I'd be able to recognize the individual trees the apples came from. They know me still. Their energy meets mine with a kiss. I am crushed by the memory of two summers past, when Amy and I put in a new herb patch at the farm. She lent me her pipe when we smoked on the porch. Called me Hard-hitter.

I've gotten too used to dreaming my days away. I've lost the thread of conversation, and only pick it up again once I hear my name.

"Sorry, but are we sure Julian is fit to take part, given her condition?" Hetal says.

Amy rounds on her, jabs her pipestem at my chest. "She's right there! You can ask her yourself."

"I don't think I'm being unreasonable here."

"Yeah?"

Hetal rolls her eyes and I feel...absolutely nothing. I grope around inside myself, in the place my sense of annoyance should be, but annoyance has passed me by. My chest is full of clouds.

The smoke from Amy's pipe thickens into a violet coagulation, falling to the ground in tendrils. Hetal's expression remains aloof, even as the Cup-a-Soup in her lap boils over the lip of her camping thermos.

Witches' emotions are dangerous. That's why I keep mine bundled in a quarter-inch ball in my right lung.

"I've got a pad of paper!" says Sato. She has it in my hands before anyone can react, and retreats to the other side of the campfire.

I write:

"merry met, Hetal. i can fight. my magic isn't as strong without words, but i can use my will to similar effect."

I finish the note with a smiley face, for extra reassurance.

Hetal takes the note. She doesn't look convinced by what she reads; I can't really blame her. I've been an oratory witch as long as I've been a witch of any kind. Everyone's got their knack, their own way to tap into their magic. For Marissa it's baking, Sato sings. Hetal's a fire witch. I talk my powers into action. Casting spells without a voice is a real handicap for me, and Hetal's just making sure I can put up a good fight. That we won't lose another friend. I flex my fingers thoughtfully, and stand.

I pick out a nearby tree. A sugar maple. This specimen looks old and healthy, its leaves faded on a gradient from yellow to burning red. Sugar maple wood is a bitch and a half to work, which is exactly what I'm looking for.

I scoop up a fallen birch twig as thick as my ring finger and brittle as a saltine cracker. Behind me, the coven falls silent.

First, I address the twig in my mind: *Hey, you. Rise, ready yourself.* The stick lifts from my palm to hover in the air at nose height. Now for the difficult bit.

Jabforwardpierce. I have to make the thoughts fast to make the spell fast. It zings. The twig pelts forward into the tree, 'smack' as it connects like a softball hit out of the park, biting deep. The coven gives a collective murmur of approval. Sato even claps. I bow and recover the twig, presenting it to her with a flourish.

"See?" Amy barks, "And if she could talk, you bet that would have bored a hole straight through the heartwood! She's fine."

It's too emphatic. I'm missing something.

"Amy," says Hetal, "I mean no ill will."

Amy's mouth twists. She's going to say something she'll regret. Hetal can see it too, so she holds a hand out over the fire and says:

"Peace be on this gathering."

It's an old blessing. The words blanket the group in calm, make the campfire burn brighter. Hetal breathes out slowly and offers her hand to me. She has woken the magic in her bones, the witch's equivalent of revving an engine, and my own witchcraft flares in response. When I got magic six years ago, I woke up every morning worried it had evaporated in the night, but it was always there, as much a part of me as my ribs. Amy got hers from her mother. I got mine from Imogen. Hetal is a rare example of spontaneous generation, a gift that drew her all the way from the West coast to train at Wells Farm. She's never held that over any of us, that she's special.

I take her hand. Our magics burn against each other, hers a marigold orange, mine the color of sunlight caught in a jar of honey. Our bones show through our brown skin, lit from within, deep in the marrow. Like the most beautiful x-ray you could imagine. Hetal studies me.

"You don't have to fight, Julian," she says. "I don't know if anyone's told you that yet. I've always respected you, and that hasn't changed." She glances pointedly at Amy. "But no one here wants to see you hurt."

It's too late for that.

Amy scowls as our witch-fires retreat, then gives her wrist a distracted shake to blow out the last spark of her own leaf-green magic. She looks like she wants to tell me something. Six months ago I would have been able to hazard a guess as to what, but I've been gone that whole time, and I don't know if—

"Julian?" Hetal prompts me.

I take out the waitress pad. Hetal reads what I write, then nods her acceptance.

"If you're sure" she says.

***

The coven settles into camp as the first stars make their appearance. The twins drop by my one-man tent and tap on the mosquito netting.

"Amy wants a word," Kendra says, "in private. *Finally.*"

"It took her forever to work up the guts to go get you in the first place."

"She pretty much crapped herself, is how I'd describe it."

"Accurate."

I shoo them off and find Amy smoking by the brook at the edge of camp. Did she always smoke so much? The tips of her nails are stained brown, but that's just Amy, never bothering with gloves when she gardens. Her eyes won't meet mine.

"I'm glad you decided to come along for this, Julian."

I give her a thumbs up.

"Yeah, so, I'm just gonna be honest. I don't know how to say what I want to say. It's, you know," she glares at the brook like it's criticized her compost heap, "it's difficult."

She holds out her hand, with something cupped in the palm. It's a human tooth, smooth, the color of old piano keys. A memory from Anatomy lessons long past whispers that it's a bicuspid. Amy taps it with her finger and it splits down the middle into two even pieces, exposing the pulp.

At the center of the tooth is an unmistakable amber glow. If you sawed my bones in half, you'd find the same glow nesting inside. And I know without a doubt who that tooth belonged to.

"It's the only new lead we've had while you've been away. When Claudia brought this back from her scouting mission, I knew I had to tell you. So you could be there for the fight, if you wanted."

She hands me the tooth. I don't know what to do with my face.

Thankfully, neither does Amy. We sit together in our shared awkwardness, and I think to myself that anger might be the only negative emotion I miss. There's something to be said for a stomach full of righteous anger. I brush Amy's shoulder as I leave. I take the tooth with me.

***

We ride in Catherine's van to the bog site first thing in the morning. A couple flying witches are easy enough to magic from view, but twelve of us, zipping along in v formation like so many geese, would be harder to manage. We're crammed in elbow to crotch, quiet the whole way, except for the click of Anita's knitting needles. She's knitting pure magic, spells that float and feather invisibly in the air of the van. I wind a silky strand around my finger. Amy gathers fistfuls of protection spells into her lap.

"Suit up, everyone," she grunts.

What follows is an amusing interlude of witches shuffling around and wrapping invisible ribbons of spell anywhere they can make them stick: around their wrists, twisted through their hair. Sato ties hers around her chest like a bungee harness. We would look absolutely wild to any outside viewer.

Catherine parks us at a point off the road that doesn't seem any different from the rest of the idyllic forestland. The coven splits, fanning out around the bog's central pond. As I approach the water's edge, the ground under my feet begins to squelch. The air has a dirty/clean quality to it, like a mud mask in a fancy spa. Hemlock trees give way to larches, and azaleas to blueberry bushes.

Kettle bogs are glacier-scooped holes in the ground, filled with water, edged with moss, and teeming with boggy life. The sphagnum moss forms floating mats thick enough to walk on. I've tried it. It's not for the faint-hearted. The moss wobbles like a water-bed, and the whole time you're remembering that if you misplace a step, or press down too hard, you could wind up trapped beneath the mat, alone in the wet and the dark.

Magically speaking, kettle bogs are liabilities, powerhouses so invested in their own balance that any invasion, any little upset, gets pulled in and worked over until it, too, becomes part of the bog.

Sometimes people fall into bogs and die. Sometimes they don't die. It may happen that they find themselves sucked into a cataract in the water, where the moss grows greener and the bullfrogs hunt. There, caught between life and death and snared by deep magic, they will be made to fit. They will be tapped into a force of nature, and they will be hungry.

Catherine points. I see it now, crouching on a mat near the center of the pool, a sized-up version of the dead one I found floating in the Green River years ago.

Frogmen aren't some Lovecraftian impossibility, a profanity against nature that sears your eyeballs dry. They're horrible to look at because they're so damn plausible. They're exactly how you'd imagine. You see one, you think, 'Yeah. Okay.' Like you wouldn't be surprised to find one on a missing page of a biology textbook: 'Rana homina, mankind's amphibious cousin.' Six feet of cold skin, big old eyes, a giant bullfrog with a face that hints at its human origins. A monster, but a believable one.

We have it surrounded. Amy whistles like a goldfinch, a party trick she picked up from her dark past as the world's grumpiest Daisy Scout. So we begin.

First up is the 'just shoot it' test. The barrel of Gabriela's lever-action hunting rifle peeks between the boughs of a nearby spruce. It'll be best if this all ends before we have to break out the magic. If the frogman's not in full control of his powers yet, that might be possible. A bullet to the temple will kill just about anything.

It's seen her.

The frogman turns his golden saucer eye to Gabriela's hiding place. His cheeks flare soundlessly. Gabriela pulls the trigger—squelch.

The gun doesn't fire. Two fruitless squelches later, and I see the problem: a patch of muddied sphagnum trails from the tip of the barrel. It wasn't there a second ago. I imagine there's more moss stuffed up against the hammer, a chamber of bullets turned to cranberries. Gabby reacts more sensibly than I might, flicking on the safety and tossing the rifle away.

There's no doubt in my mind that if we weren't wearing Anita's protection charms, we'd all be gagging on wads of moss already. He's come into the fullness of his powers, and he knows we're here. Guns won't be enough.

Amy gestures at me to give it a shot, so I try the twig trick. The twig is turned to moss before it gets within twelve feet of him. It hits his chest with a wet sound.

"All right, good to know..."

Amy reaches into her coat and draws out a fat, leather pouch like the kind kids keep their marbles in. The side's labeled in Sharpie: 'Home Field Advantage.' It's filled with soil samples from every corner of her farm. We say 'dirt poor' or 'dirty'—we don't give soil the respect it deserves. Amy does, and that's why it listens to her. It carries her magic. She opens the pouch, licks her thumb, and coats it with dirt. Pops her thumb in her mouth like she's taking a pinch of snuff. She always does that; I can never get over it.

"Yeah," she murmurs, "that should do it."

Amy casts a fistful of dirt over the sphagnum mat. *She blows a smoke ring from her pipe, breathes it out to mix with the dust in the air. Smoke ignites dust into a wicked gout of green fire, sucking in air and cannoning it back out with a crack, all the way across the surface of the bog. The frogman shrieks. The tops of my braids singe.*

"*Boom,*" says Amy, like she's cool. Her accompanying grin almost makes it so. This is her declaration of war. The ragged patches of burned flesh on the frogman's cheek heal near instantly, but they existed. Amy did damage to him. She's proven it's possible, even now.

She tries again, this time whistling to Hetal to join in. Hetal's fire is hotter, more focused, striking out from the other side of the bog. I'm sure that, between Hetal and Amy, the frogman's not going to be up for another round. When the twin fires fall away, I see that I'm wrong. The frogman emerges unscathed from a mound of steaming sphagnum. He licks his own eyeball.

"Shit," Amy hisses, "we're going to have to send out Sato."

We all tease Sato about her water-walking. She's the sort of Catholic who doesn't mind a joking comparison to Jesus. She sings her magic into power in her flutey soprano, sweet and forceful. Anita watches and twists knots into her skein of invisible yarn, her lips pressed bloodlessly together. We don't want Sato to die. She shouldn't be here, really. She hasn't even finished college. A feeling that is almost unease presses against my throat... and down into my lung. Poof. At ease again.

I still care about Sato.

I had to check to be sure.

Her magic pushes against the frogman's pebbled hide, and because her attack is force itself, not a tangible object, he cannot turn it into a part of his bog. Invisible fingers press at his clammy throat. The pulse there pounds, blue blood close to the surface, ready to pop. His back legs twitch. The water under Sato lurches and roils, sending the moss mats undulating, but she steps calmly over each wave. The frogman raises another cocoon of mats to protect himself. Sato shivers it apart. She's close enough to touch him now, her song relentless and sweet. Another eight-count should finish him. He kicks weakly. He opens his mouth wide.

Faster than my eyes can follow, a pink blur of a tongue shoots past the frogman's lips and grabs Sato around her outstretched hand. It snaps her to his jaws. Sato doesn't stop singing. She weaves her screams into her song, even as her arm is crushed, even as her legs give out in pain.

I blink and Amy's gone.

I taste ozone in the back of my mouth.

Amy stands on a platter-sized lump of hardened mud, her right arm raised above her head, palm out like she's blocking the sun. Blue blood runs over her face. The tip of a severed tongue floats on the surface of the pond. And oh, the frogman is angry. The magic in the air is sharp with it.

"Scatter," Amy rasps. Sato doesn't have to be told twice. She dashes back to the shore so fast her feet barely brush the water, and when she stumbles, her song finally faltering as she runs out of breath, Anita tugs her the rest of the way by yanking on the protection charm.

We all know that Amy's meant to be the last line of defense. She says "Scatter" again, then yells it, and that's the cue for us all to get out, to get far away. Everyone else obeys her like they should. But what do I have to lose, really? Only Amy. Only myself. I'm willing to fight for one of those things, at least. I swim out to them. Amy and the frogman are locked in a motionless battle of wills. It looks as if nothing magical is happening at all, but Amy's gone white as milk and the frogman is twitching again. Anything could happen.

My magic slides off of him like beads of oil.

"Julian," Amy chokes, and somehow, even fighting a losing battle against a monster, she gives my name that same note of frustration she always does. The frogman pulls her to his chest, and sinks.

Down he goes. Down Amy goes, the flailing stump of her pinky finger the last bit of her to be dragged below the mat, and then it's gone.

What do I do? My will isn't enough. I've never felt like I'm enough. Knowing that hurts me, right now, and all my other emotions rush in with that pain, because I've already made my decision.

All those months I spent silent, and I don't even know what word I break my spell with. I scream a shapeless nonsense. The pain blooms out from my chest, a ring of red, and the only reason I know it's not just happening in my head is the smell of bog water flash-evaporating.

The pain eats me whole.

***

It's a simple spell, the one I cast in April. The different names sound like flowers: "Heart-in-a-Box", "Consolation," "Mary's Breath." Imogen cast it when her mother died. I cast it when Imogen died.

She told me, "I don't think we're supposed to live like that for long. I regretted it after." But what did she know? She died and left us all behind.

Burn something you love. Breathe in the ash. The particles will form a clump in your lung, a ball of pain and ash and magic, pressed so tight together that it takes ages for it to grow to any significant size. But it does grow. It's where your pain goes. Some witches have kept the spell going so long that they choke on it. Some must have wanted to let it go, but the pain was too much to ever take back safely. Because it doesn't go away, that's not the point. You are borrowing distance from it. Still it remains yours, forever and ever, amen.

Don't speak.

When Imogen went missing last spring, I didn't believe she was dead until we found her right foot at the bottom of a vernal pool in Hopkins Forest. Tadpoles were nibbling at the flesh, a wriggling halo.

I could handle that, nearly. I handled it for weeks. What I couldn't handle was the argument outside the coffee shop on Spring Street, when Amy admitted that we may never know what exactly had happened. Imogen was taken by some snarl of magic powerful enough to make my eyes water, but it wasn't like magic as Imogen had pictured it, as she had shown me in the Stop and Shop break room during lunch, braiding heal-all and rushes together into a charm to warm our hands. She loved magic, she loved the forest, and it killed her.

Which part?

Outside the coffee shop, I said, *"Leave me alone, Amy,"* spell-tinged, the first time I'd worked magic against her. She took a step back.

"Julian," she said.

I couldn't think of anything else to say.

"She was my friend, too," she told me.

That didn't help. Even though I knew it was true, even though some distant piece of myself could see that Amy was wrecked, her lips gnawed red at the corners.

I'd kissed her once. That's what I remembered, looking at her then. All she wanted was my patience, but I didn't have any. We were both so tired.

I still couldn't think of anything to say. That's when I decided I was going to use the spell. Never speaking again didn't seem like such a sacrifice in that moment. I would leave, I would be quiet, I wouldn't hurt so bad.

I wouldn't hurt at all.

***

This wasn't what I signed up for when Imogen offered to share her magic with me. I think I loved her then, this focused arrow of a girl, beaming in the honeyed glow like a kid sharing a secret. I could see she'd been dying to show me for weeks, maybe since we talked on my first shift at the store. I was new to the Berkshires, and everything felt possible, even magic. I wanted to believe her. We met at night in the snowy woods behind my dorm. She showed me fire conjured to a candle at will: candle off, candle on. The littlest trick, and I was hooked.

"You can have this too, if you want," she said. "It's not giving you something new, it's lighting up something you already have."

"Will I be able to do the same things you can?"

"Maybe, but it'll never be exactly the same. It's different for every person. Like, the same flame burning from different candles. Personally, I think you'd be a good witch. You just have to promise. There's a thing we say."

"Hit me with it."

"I promise," she began.

"I promise," I repeated.

"...not to be a total asshole."

I raised my eyebrows, and Imogen held up her hands.

"Hey, Amy's words, not mine," she said.

"I do like Amy."

"I'll be sure to tell her."

"But you know, it's fair enough. I promise not to be a total asshole."

"Now we hold hands."

There's no way I can describe what it feels like to catch witch-fire. To have your bones light up. It's so glorious you think you'll keel over, but you don't. The weight of what you've been given holds you steady, and who'd want to be an asshole with that joy? Who'd even be tempted?

"Merry met, Julian," said Imogen.

I answered, "Merry met, Imogen," and the light around us fractured beautifully at the sound of my voice. I could almost hear an echo: *Merry, merry...Imogen.*

"Oh man," she said, "okay, you might having a speaking specialty! Tell your candle to light."

"*Candle,*" I commanded, "*Light.*"

It did. It caught fire like anything. We jumped up and down until the snow around us was crushed into slurry, and then we jumped some more.

I kept the stump of that candle with me for years, until it was time to burn something I loved.

***

I come to with the taste of candle smoke in my mouth. I'm under the bog, I think, in a red-lit world where every movement hurts. Amy hangs in mid-air above me, un-moving. No water here, just the memory of water. The frogman floats across from me, stunned. I know I have no time. Soon this bubble of pent-up magic will collapse as the bog works to bring itself back into balance. I gather Amy up, swimming through the pain like it's syrup. Then I face the frogman, wet my lips, and speak.

"You can talk if you want, I bet. Did you kill the witch Imogen Gillespie? *Talk.*"

It's the first thing I've said in months; the screaming doesn't feel like it counts. Just when I decide I can't wait any longer, the frogman's mouth opens.

"Ribbit," he whispers. The onomatopoeic word, not the sound. I can't tell if it's a joke or not, there's no way to know. Which would be worse? His jelly eyes are flat and cold. They tell me nothing. I'm out of time.

"Your skull cracks." It does, I hear the crunch. *"You die."* Simple, and I believe it. I leave, swimming to the surface.

Someday I'll come back for Imogen's bones.

* * *

I burst through the surface of the bog. The water's back where it should be. A dragonfly drifts past. I tread water, take advantage of my newly reclaimed voice so I can swear, and grab for a floating larch branch. Anything can be a broom in a pinch if you're panicked enough.

"You're a broom," I tell it. It lifts me and Amy out of the muck so fast I gag, but we're gone, and I'm going to try to help her.

We land near a river half a mile away. I drag us toward the shore. My arms blister with nettle stings and the claw marks of barberry shrubs. Pain is so alien now, each prickle shocks me to the heart. I scramble out of the undergrowth to a beach of river rocks. I sweep them off bare-handed to find the sand underneath. Amy doesn't stir from the patch of coltsfoot I've set her on, not even when I rifle through her pockets for her bags of precious dirt.

I cover the stretch of sand with the last of Home Field Advantage, turning the bag inside-out to get the last grains of earth. I don't know if it's enough. Amy would know.

The river's rushing, cold, deep enough to push Amy under. I hold her down with a granite stone on her belly, and I'm crying so hard my eyes itch. Dark silt pours from her lips. I give her twenty seconds, then I roll the rock aside. Up she bobs to the surface. Now the darkness is just an ink-spot here and there on her pink skin.

She's heavier than she was before, like all the snowmelt in the Berkshires is resting in her stomach. By the time I've got her laid out onto her bed of sand and dirt, everything is scattered all to hell.

"Help her," I say. A spell.

I swallow. The soil does nothing. It wants to help, I can tell. The whispers it sends back to me are desperate to mend, to soothe, to move. The dirt knows me, but I'm not its mistress. A pouch by my feet stirs. I reach for it without thinking, and it jumps into the palm of my hand. The label reads: 'Julian's Herb Patch.'

"Help us," I tell it. Holding it makes me feel better.

I reach for Amy's witch-fire. I think, 'Same flame, two different candles.' All of us witches bound together by that one thing, in life and death. I say,

"You know me. We're going to do this together. Show me where the problem is."

Her bones light up that chilly spring green. There, in her chest, is a lump of silt-black magic that's definitely not Amy's.

"Black lump. Bog magic. Ease yourself out. You're going to leave through the least damaging path."

It's sudden. Amy rears up, eyes streaming, and coughs grotesquely. I turn her towards the river. Plop. A piece of nature returned to nature, and good riddance. It dissolves into fir needles.

"Hey," she manages. Her voice is shredded and will be for weeks.

Through the gap in the trees, I see ten distant spots in the sky. Our coven safe and together. Our coven coming for us. I collapse in the grit. Everything hurts, is gonna keep hurting, but—

"Amy."

"Yeah?"

"Nothing. I'm just enjoying the sound of your name."

That flusters her a bit. Her ears flush, and I happily imagine the little blood cells getting on with their business, carrying oxygen to her extremities, everything ticking along just as it should. She's not so pale now.

"I want to kiss you."

It's amazing being able to say that, to sound out the words and see her reaction.

"I mean you can, but why would you want to, I'm absolutely gross right now."

She tastes like a mud pie, and I only care a little.

"Yeah, you taste like dirt."

"Julian," she says, in that way she has.

Star Bound

Devon Widmer

Grumpy graduate student by day.
Scribbling daydreamer by night. Sleep
deprived parent full-time. Currently,
Devon Widmer is meandering down
a long, winding road toward a PhD in
physical chemistry. Her talents include
drinking copious amounts of coffee,
forgetting where she set her glasses, and
laughing at her own jokes.

After ripping off her welding helmet and swiping a gloved hand across her grimy forehead, Terra sighed in sweaty relief. Personal protective equipment was oh so necessary but oh so constricting.

Stepping back, she examined her work. It wasn't the cleanest joint she'd ever welded, but it would hold a few million megaparsecs. Far enough to get to the university in time for Vivi's conference. Terra would never be able to forgive herself if Vivi missed delivering the keynote speech on account of her old rust bucket of a starship. She rapped a fist against the metal hull—*clang!*—and grinned. The old girl still had a bit of life in her. Then, more lovingly, Terra reached out to trace the letters her mother had engraved on the vessel's side when Terra was only fourteen. *Star Bound.* A fitting name for a homemade starship built by a girl and her mom in the slums of Gaia Nine, a starship that only two people had ever really expected to fly. That was the kind of mom Terra wanted to be. An unstoppable force ready to knock back all the so-called immovable objects life dropped in her own daughter's path.

After slipping off her insulated gloves, Terra rubbed her midsection absentmindedly. A button, having strained admirably over the past few months to hold the stiff fabric of her jumpsuit around her expanding belly, popped off beneath her fingers. Terra fiddled with the frayed buttonhole.

She wasn't ready.

Not remotely.

A wave of nausea surged upward, through Terra's stomach and into her chest, where it bubbled and burned. She leaned against the starship and breathed. Maybe she didn't *have* to be a fantastic mom. After all, she'd gotten out. Her own mom had made sure of *that*, snarling past every condescending acquaintance and misguided educator who claimed little girls from backwater planets simply weren't cut out for the Intergalactic Science and Engineering Academy. *Star Bound* wasn't a distant dream anymore but Terra's daily reality. The nausea drained back down to the pit of her stomach, fizzling to a bearable simmer. Maybe it was ok to just be ok—the corners of Terra's eyes crinkled ever so slightly—and at least she wasn't in this adventure alone.

"*Terra! Terraaaa!*"

Terra whipped around just in time to see Vivi burst from the underbrush a few meters away, tripping over her own feet as she scrambled toward the landing site. Snatching up her welding torch, Terra darted around the ship, ready to blast whatever beast had dared to terrorize her wife.

But when Vivi stumbled into Terra's frantic embrace, her eyes, framed by clumps of sopping wet hair, sparkled not with fear but excitement. "Wanna see something *incredible?*"

***

Terra shooed a fat insectoid from her nose before grinding her fists against her hips. Her wetsuit stretched tight across her tummy and pinched her tender breasts, which had swelled almost a full cup size larger than the last time she'd gone diving with Vivi—pregnancy hormones were a pain in the, well, boob.

"Hurry in—the water's fantastic!" Vivi laughed and splashed as if swimming in a chilly, extraterrestrial lagoon at sunset was a real party. And, for Dr. Vivian Huang, academic superstar and author of *the* textbook on marine astroherpetology, it basically *was* a party.

A begrudging smile pulled at the corners of Terra's mouth. She preferred the familiar sweat, grit, and oil of her machine shop, but Vivi's enthusiasm for fieldwork was too infectious to resist. After closing her eyes and scrunching up her face, Terra stepped tentatively forward. "*Huah!*" She gasped as her toe broke the water's surface. "It's f-freezing."

"Only when you first get in."

That was a damn lie.

But when Vivi's fingers wove comfortably into her own, Terra hardly noticed the cold.

"Missed one." Vivi tucked a stray ringlet under Terra's diving cap as the two tread water. "There." Her eyes, wide with excitement and a tiny twinge of worry, sparkled in the light of double moons. "Sure you feel up to this, dear? I don't want you overexerting yourself."

After rolling her eyes, Terra dipped underwater to puff her cheeks full of water, which she then playfully squirted in Vivi's face. "I'm pregnant, not ill, ya dingus." Then, before Terra could finish blinking, a splash of cold water broke across her own face.

"I know, I know—but I'll fuss over you all the same."

Terra buzzed her lips and then, grinning, dried her eyes on her sleeve. "Fair enough."

"I promise this won't take long. Then we can snuggle back in the ship. I'll brew you some of that ginger tea you love so much."

Terra grimaced. "You know I only drink that stuff to ward off morning sickness."

"Then judging by our dwindling supply of chocolate bars, I'd say it's working a little too well."

Though Terra made a show of sticking out her tongue, she reveled in the way the sunburnt freckles on Vivi's nose wrinkled when she laughed.

"Ready?" Vivi held out a small packet of bright blue gel. "We don't need to go deep—promise. Just a few meters. Nothing dangerous for you. Or for baby girl."

Terra accepted the proffered packet and then gently placed it under her tongue. The water-soluble outer membrane dissolved within seconds. Terra inhaled, grimacing as the breathing jelly filled her lungs. Then she thrust her face into the water to suck in a few short breaths. Satisfied, she flashed Vivi a thumbs up.

Together, they dived.

***

With two moons shimmering from above and the glow of phosphorescent weeds below, the lagoon was surprisingly well lit. Kicking deftly to the bottom, Vivi scooped up a handful of the glowing leaves. After tying a few around her own wrists, she draped the rest around Terra's shoulders like a shawl and planted a kiss on her forehead. Then, with an effortless backstroke, Vivi zipped nimbly ahead.

Terra followed, flailing her arms and legs. She grinned. So what if "intoxicated frog" was her only swim stroke? It was a nice change from the pregnant "penguin waddle" she'd begun developing on land. Smiling serenely, she swept her arms in broad, graceful strokes and—*thnk!*—head-butted a rock.

After straightening up to rub her head, Terra scanned the lagoon floor for Vivi. She spied her a few meters away, hovering at the edge of a wide trench. The glowing reeds tied to Vivi's wrists twirled through the water like dancing ribbons as she gestured excitedly downward. Terra flutter-kicked over. Curling her fingers over the edge, she peered down into...darkness. A *lot* of darkness. Terra shot Vivi a raised eyebrow. Winking cryptically, Vivi unwrapped a reed from her wrist, knotted it, and then dropped the glowing ball into the trench. It drifted downward, illuminating the pockmarked rock walls until—Terra saw it.

Coils. Writhing coils. Writhing coils weaving into even more writhing coils, a seemingly endless mass, spinning, winding, undulating. For an instant, the glisten of white teeth and golden eyes flashed before burrowing out of sight. A shiver threatening to slip down Terra's spine but she held her shoulders rigid. The creepy, crawly creatures of the universe's oceans were decidedly *not* her cup of tea. But Vivi simply adored them. A slender arm slipped around Terra's shoulder and she could feel her wife practically vibrating with excitement.

As their eyes met, Vivi rolled her fingers in front of her face in the sign for "Beautiful." Terra curled her lips into what she hoped was more smile than grimace. Vivi signed more vigorously. "Beautiful—beautiful." Then, after a pause, she clarified with a thumb against her chin, "Momma. Beautiful momma."

Terra's heart fluttered. She squinted back down into the darkness. Vivi's phosphorescent reed ball had long faded, presumably crushed within those churning coils. Terra slipped a weed from her shoulders before smashing it into a clumsy wad. With a slightly trembling hand, she released the wad. It spiraled down, down, down as it fell. There it was again, the snake-like sea monster, and...there! Vivi's fingernails dug into Terra's shoulders as a red, distended balloon snaked into view. The bulge pulsed like a heartbeat and, from within, dark shadows wriggled.

Vivi shook Terra's shoulders before signing, "Beautiful momma, like you," and beamed.

Terra cocked her head a moment but then, cheeks flushing, buried her face in her hands. Her body shook as fat bubbles of laughter slipped past her lips. Under any other circumstances, she would have resented being compared to a giant writhing sea monster full of giant writhing sea monster spawn, but coming from Dr. Vivian "Giant Writhing Sea Monsters Are My Passion" Huang, that was actually a heartfelt compliment. No wonder Vivi had been so eager to drag her pregnant wife on an underwater monster observation mission.

After recovering from her giggling fit, Terra reached up to twine her fingers into Vivi's. Vivi squeezed Terra's hand tightly and leaned her head against Terra's shoulder. And so, hand-in-hand, they lay on the precipice's edge, taking turns dropping down weed-balls to observe the monstrous mother-to-be.

***

After a few guttural coughs, Terra spit the last of her breathing jelly onto the shore. As the gel beaded, sparkling amongst the grains of sand as electric blue spheres, she drew a deep, satisfying breath of air.

Beside her, Vivi peeled off her diving cap. "It'll be a live birth." Her fingers fluffed her short black hair. "Like some of the ancient marine reptiles of Gaia One. And any day now by the looks of it. Oh gosh—" She twirled on tippy-toes with her arms flung wide before flopping onto her back in the sand. "—what I wouldn't give to stay and observe her."

Terra twisted her head from side to side, thumping the heel of her hand against one ear, then the other. She felt...ok. Not great. But ok. Try as she might, she couldn't get the image of the sea monster's bulbous red belly and writhing black spawn from her mind. Perhaps because the chilly swim had woken up the writhing monster in her own belly. *Kick. Kick. Kick.* It was a wonder those thunderous little feet hadn't yet burst through her thin stretched skin. What must that sea monster feel with at least half a dozen mini monsters bashing against that taut red balloon belly? And how strange was it to empathize with an extraterrestrial sea monster?

"So," she said, stretching before plopping down onto the sand next to Vivi, "let's stay."

"Can't." Vivi flailed her arms and legs like a toddler in the throws of a tantrum. "Conference."

"Skip it."

Vivi's eyes widened, almost hopeful, but then her lips curled back in a grimace. "Terra, I'm the *keynote speaker*. You can't skip a conference when you're the keynote speaker."

"Lucy can give the speech," said Terra with a shrug. Lucy. Dr. Lucille Burns. Vivi's former graduate student and current post-doc. "It'd be a good opportunity for her. Besides which, between all your faculty meetings, grant writing, and freshman

Introduction to Biology office hours, she's probably done more of the *actual* work for the paper you're presenting." She smirked. Vivi didn't. "Only joking about that last bit—I for one should know how many ungodly hours you spend holed up in your lab."

"It's not that." Vivi still wasn't smiling. Instead, she stroked her chin between her thumb and forefinger.

"Then what?"

"It's just—well, I did actually already contact Lucy to prep her for the speech. You know, after we...." She spiraled a hand downwards while whistling and then pounding her fist into the sand. "Just in case you couldn't fix the ship in time—even though of course I *never* doubted you'd fix the ship in time. You know that old, er, *seasoned* ship inside-out and upside-down." She paused, thinking, then rolled onto her side and batted her eyes in an obnoxious imitation of casual. "I mean, I'm sure you've already fixed the ship, haven't you, my darling?"

Terra smiled with her eyes and frowned with her mouth. "Actually, dear, I've been meaning to talk to you about that. The repairs simply haven't gone to plan. I expect they'll take a few more days, maybe even a few more weeks."

"Good heavens! That's simply awful news." Vivi grinned. "I cannot see how I could possibly make the conference now."

"Such a shame. I do know how you were looking forward to those many, many hours crammed into lecture halls with people who've spent more time socializing with globs of algae in tests tubes than with actual human beings."

"I happen to *be* one of those people, thank you very much, and I was actually looking forward to it." Vivi squirmed closer to Terra and nuzzled her face into the crook of Terra's neck. "But," she whispered, "I'm looking even *more* forward to some impromptu field research with my blossoming family." While nibbling the lobe of Terra's ear, Vivi cradled an arm around Terra's stomach, which jiggled as the baby let out another massive kick. "Oh!" Vivi shot up, her eyes wide. "She kicked! Baby kicked!"

Terra rolled lazily onto her side and propped her head up with her arm. "She's *been* kicking. My innards are probably all black and blue."

"Our little martial artist," cooed Vivi, resting her ear against Terra's stomach. Terra's fingers curled almost instinctively into Vivi's short hair. As she teased the smooth strands between her fingers, Vivi tilted her head to gaze admiringly up. "You're gonna be a great mom. You know that, right?"

Terra paused, chewing her lower lip. "Eh. I'll be ok."

"Not ok. Great. You're gonna be great."

Something about the earnestness in Vivi's eyes stilled Terra's protest. Instead, after a brief pause and a flash of teeth, she corrected, "*We're* gonna be great."

Vivi lifted her head and then wriggled up to plant a kiss on Terra's forehead. Then one on each cheek. And, lastly, a nice sloppy wet one on her lips. "Yeah," she murmured. "Yeah, we are."

After a deep, contented sigh, Vivi and Terra turned their gazes upward. There would be a lot of work in the coming weeks—contacting Vivi's graduate students, setting up a base camp, arranging shipment for all of the necessary equipment—but right now, all Terra wanted to do was lie her on this extraterrestrial beach, limbs intertwined with her wife's, and gaze at the twinkling stars above.

Radio, out by Pluto

Lydia Pauly

Lydia is a U.K. based science fiction
writer, who works with exclusively
female, android, or alien characters.
Outside of writing, she's a political
researcher and comfortable wallflower.

In darkness, far beyond the warmth of the Sun, a tiny satellite crawled across the face of Pluto. Suspended in orbit, it sailed in the quiet vacuum, a thin stream of data ebbing back and forth between the craft and the surface probe at the equator, similar to dust motes in an updraft.

On board, clicking in an otherwise silent chamber, a slow graph etched across a screen, then erased itself to repeat. On the opposite side, numbers in fine lettering trickled across and out of view. Cold, sterile air, with the temperature settling around 1 degree Celsius, breathed stagnant out of the filter system, dry and thin. Across the terminals, a fine dust of frost had crystallised, splitting the low light of Pluto into a fragile spectrum of colour.

The Processor sat at the control desk, unmoving, limbs cast in green from the glow of the screens. She had her hands out in front of her, spread like metal starfish across the terminal, the digits of each finger slotted into circular electrical ports. Through these contacts, the raw data from Pluto's surface fed into her body and flowed out again, cleaned, checked, then taken back for analysis. She sat there for fifteen hours.

After this time had passed, the Processor rose and touched her hands to the earthing rod to remove the static. A gentle buzz disturbed the room, before it fell back into ambiance. She left and climbed up into her personal chamber: a functional bed, and a mirror. She sat before it, and inspected her body from her toes to her ears, her fingers ringing taps against her titanium body. She took the glass plates that covered her eyes, the only organic part of her left behind. She checked them once, then twice again. The whites were bloodshot. Perhaps the frigid air is an irritant, she thought. I'll have to keep an eye on them. Thinking that, she paused in surprise, then smiled to no one.

Before she went back in for recharge, the Processor made her way to the bottom of the satellite, entering into a dark room, less polished than the data processing space. Twists of metal and wiring were collected on the floor, coloured tubing in all the primary colours, piling up towards a terminal in the middle of the room. The screen flickered: an old-style monitor that still used cathode tubes.

She pressed a button on the side of the screen. The screen refreshed. A timer ticked over on the bottom left hand side: fifty Earth years and counting.

The Processor stood back up and looked out through the window at the top of the craft. An asteroid-marked dish was mounted on the side of the satellite and pointed away from Pluto, battered and twisted away from the normal architecture of the ship. When she'd first mounted it, she leant out of a decompressed chamber out into the dark itself, with a legacy helmet sealed to her neck with electrical tape. She remembered the dizziness of it. Even though the gravity was turned off, she still held onto the sides as she stretched out and rammed the neck of the dish into its drilled hole. As if she might fall, pulled down by something impossibly large that swam beneath her. Over the years, little pieces of rock from the system had knocked against it, but it was still there, bolted in with screws salvaged from other, less important parts of the ship.

That had been fifty years ago, she thought. And still, nothing back.

She pressed another button on the side of the screen. The message, crackled and full of static, barely audible in the deoxygenated room: her voice—her lost, organic voice—humming over Bach's *Prélude in G Major*.

Leaning against the monitor, the Processor thought about her voice, echoing out past through the stars. On it would go, until eventually the radio waves were absorbed into rocks and other, lonely planets, lost into inanimate objects. And yet, she thought. For such a lonely mission, it lets the years go by a little less painfully.

***

Another twenty Earth years passed, quietly.

The Processor had her hands on the contacts, eyes closed, her internal processors put to their primary use. Outside, the blue of Pluto was waxing, slipping down below the viewing window as the satellite spun back towards the Sun. When she finally raised her hands again, she let them rest in her lap. She was surprised by how heavy she felt. Tired? *No*, she thought. *Exhausted, is what I would have called it.* She looked down at herself, the metal joins at her knuckles worn and scratched. *Does a concept like that even make sense anymore?* she wondered. *To someone who has no blood?*

Achingly slow, she raised herself, and climbed back up to her bed. Leaning back, the exhaustion seemed to grow, feeling as though an impossibly heavy fog was pressing against her. Sleep, she thought. Then, correcting herself: recharging. Turning to her side, she reeled out a tube from the bedside and blew air into the socket on her neck to clean the port. It itched when it shouldn't.

Tomorrow, she thought. The heaviness pressed down her ability to think, making her strangely calm. The dreams would be dark and murky, almost all but forgotten by the time she woke up again. And maybe, whatever is happening will have passed. She pushed in the charging cord.

As the pre-charging routines clicked through their normal cycles, the Processor turned to the window. To distract herself, she tried to find the Sun amongst the other stars, knowing it was an almost impossible task. As she did, she thought about Earth.

For those in organic bodies, she began to think, twenty years is the first quarter of a lifespan. In this body, what does that mean? Here, only just over a tenth of a year has passed. Hundreds have passed back home. *Whatever I remember about Earth,* she thought. *About the countries I'd visited and the people I'd known.* They would be changed. Lost, perhaps. Twenty years had gone by and taken it all, quietly, with nothing to show for it, except the click of a graph across a screen and numbers no one could read. *How does that make you feel?* the Processor asked herself. Or, where are these thoughts coming from?

The Processor picked a star that looked like it could be the Sun. It was a little brighter than the rest, but there was no way to tell. The old memory of a constellation — Orion, the hunter with his hand on the pommel of his belted sword — emerged, then faded away. That was something you could only see from home.

She turned back towards the ceiling. *I don't breathe anymore,* the thoughts continued. *I don't have a heartbeat anymore. I don't experience pregnancy or menstruation anymore. All I have are my eyes. The last human experience of time that I have.* She

64

gently touched the glass covering them and shut her eyes. A blink is a second. *That, I still have.*

She felt her body shutting down to charge. Just before, she looked out at the window towards the stars. The stars stood where they were, unchanging.

***

Another twenty Earth years passed, quietly.

Data was collected, cleaned, then analysed. The results were stored in a large black-box, held in the belly of the satellite. It was due to be delivered hundreds of years from now, shot across the system until it crashed, red-hot, into the Pacific waters.

During one year, Processor had readjusted her shoulder, and it was no longer stiff. During another, her right hand collected a large, wavering scratch down the wrist from reaching into the hull space to re-tape a faulty connection. She filled it in with the green hull paint she found in the transmission room.

The monitor continued to count, without interruption.

The exhaustion came and went. Some days, she walked as easily as when she was first cast in metal. Some days, she knelt on the floor.

Outside, the Sun was still only a bright star, far from her little satellite.

***

Another twenty Earth years passed, quietly.

The Processor sat at the analysis desk and looked out at the stars. It was not an exhausted day, but she felt uneasy in herself, as if her cybernetic body was not her own. As if phantom nerves were trying to regrow from her chest, shivering against the cold metal.

She watched the stars. Her eyes followed from one to another, picking out the brightest of them. In her mind's eye, she linked them up into her own constellations: the triangle, the acorn, the comet. Memories of home, fixed into the stars. She made and unmade patterns, moving from one point of light to the next, until she came to nothing at all. Where she expected to find the tip of a poised arrow, there was only a void where stars had once been. An unnatural darkness, an unsettling absence.

The Processor stood and pulled up the telescopic view to her left screen, channelling the feed through a battered lens tube on the roof of the craft. She could only see black upon black, the telescope too small for far-range observation.

Pushing back from the desk, she went down into the transmission room and saw that the monitor was already lit up. She stopped, holding her hands against the screen, faintly buzzing against her metal. The call alert shivered on-screen as the failing tubes glitched out. Eventually, the Processor knelt down and pressed a single button on the bottom of the unit, leaning her head against the speakers.

A thin, static started. Some barely audible notes. She adjusted the pitch, applied an anti-noise filter, but still: only two notes. Two beautiful, alien notes.

Standing, she pushed up the transmission power. Then, pulling herself up to the navigation desk, she rotated the old satellite dish towards the void, guessing at coordinates until its direction and the void matched.

Back down in the transmission room, the monitor beeped again.

The Processor listened. More static. More filters and amplification yielded three more notes, which she transposed onto the original transmission. The song came through a little more, making an air.

The Processor repeated this four more times, but no more transmissions came through. Reluctantly, she left her own transmission to run automatically, and removed herself from the room, returning to the data processing. Letting her hands rest on the contacts, she slipped back into processing, her vision fading out. This time, she kept her eyes opened, locked on the void amongst the stars. Her body felt lighter than ever.

***

Another Earth year passed, in music.

Eight more transmissions came through in this time. More notes came through, but the result was confused. Some notes replaced others. Some notes had long gaps of silence between them. Major and minor keys were put together with no order, making the music erratic and unbalanced. There was no key nor rhythm.

The Processor sent back her original transmission, as well as her own tentative music made from the notes they had sent over. She transmitted them in threes, making sure the satellite dish was fixed pointedly on the void in the sky. However, each returned transmission seemed to either ignore or misunderstand. Each was more faint static, with random notes dotted throughout the sequence.

Thinking, she tried something else: the isolated file of her own voice, matching the original melody. She waited at the transmitter for a full day, knelt against its side. The answer was only silence.

Whenever she sat back at the data processing desk, she would stare back out at the void and think. We aren't communicating because we don't share a common language, she thought. Even the music I've sent them, it has rules that I understand but they don't have enough to pull apart that same structure and use it for themselves. Not only that, she thought. But maybe they're trying to communicate their own language of music to me, which I can't parse. It could be so much longer until we even begin to figure out a common language, with only these sparse radio waves. Until then, just uselessly speaking at each other, neither of us able to listen, desperate to be understood and heard by the other. She clenched her fists at the table then looked at them, surprised. Inside, she felt nothing that could describe itself as anger. Yet, there was something in her body that remembered the actions of anger. *Why does it remember?* she asked herself. *And why do I care?*

Downstairs, the monitor announced another incoming message. The Processor returned, and let the transmission play. At first, it was more faint static, followed by a low sound, like the rumbling of earth. Gently, the Processor put her head next to the speaker, trying to pick out the noise from the thin air. It grew fainter, and she moved closer, a whispering just at the edge of her hearing. Words? Sounds? She strained to listen.

Screaming, like a tearing of steel, but cut with the sound of the throat. It split through the air and made the Processor jerk away, hard body knocking the monitor, skidding it across the floor and making transmission to skip with glitchy pops. The howling disappeared as quickly as it came, cutting out to silence.

The Processor put her hand to her chest. She had no heart left, but something remembered the sensation of fluttering and pumping. A second passed, and it disappeared, her body returning to inertia.

She stood. She felt self-conscious. The monitor began to replay the message, but she came over and cut the looping. As she did, a strange, rigid calm came over her, as if another, colder part of her psyche had just re-emerged. It looked at her transmission machine, then at the void at the stars. *Do you realise how dangerous this is?* it asked. *Do you realise what you are risking? And do you realise why?*

Outside, the darkness amongst the stars was still there. Beside her, the monitor announced another incoming message.

***

Another Earth year passed.

The five transmissions came in. Some were just repeats of what she had before, although the howling never returned. Some were nothing but static. Only one was a genuine development. She could hear what sounded like voices behind the static, but she couldn't extract anything useful from them. She could only hear their tones, low and mournful.

This time, the Processor did not respond. What had seemed so important before now seemed treacherous. She had done something without thinking; she had reached out into the darkness. And now, something was responding. Something that she didn't understand. Something that distracted her from the work that she was made for, her cold psyche reminded her.

Still, she stood by the monitor, head next to the speaker, listening to everything that came in. Somehow, no matter how ashamed she felt, she couldn't stop. Over and over, the cacophony of music, the alien calls, the stretches of incoherent static. The exhaustion came in stronger now, washing over with every transmission she listened to, until she could barely stand. Half of her would sing, at the voice of someone other than her. The other half would shudder at it and at her. And yet, her hands lingered against the controls, close enough to send out another transmission of her own.

The Processor supported herself on the top of the monitor and looked out towards the void. She imagined some ethereal form coming from her chest, reaching out and grasping for whatever being lay beyond the stars, something that went beyond language. Isn't grief universal? Isn't sadness and loneliness?

No, came the answer from inside the cold part of her mind. *Those are for you to understand on your own.*

As if in response, the monitor stayed empty and silent.

***

Another Earth year passed.

More transmissions had come through, but the Processor did not listen to them. She deleted them upon arrival, and turned off her own transmissions, de-powering the dish and collapsing it against the side of the craft. She returned to her data processing. Her days existed of the moments between analysing the surface of Pluto and her darkly dreams. They were brief. She no longer lingered, no longer visited the monitor room. She checked her body briefly. She repaired what she had to, and plugged herself in with no other thoughts. She did what she designed to do.

She no longer looked outside the window. She no longer checked the stars.

***

Another twenty Earth years passed.

At the end of this period, The Processor looked up and saw that the stars had returned. Somewhere in her chest, a heart that no longer existed tightened. She walked down to the radio room. Twenty transmissions had come through.

The first four were much of the same. More discordant notes, nestled in static. The next ten were more varied, with additional notes added in, although still with no key or rhythm. Some featured purely voices, still whispering in the background. Some, the Processor thought as she listened, were even an attempt at singing. The last three were tentative, hazy attempts at actual music; still broken and scattered, but the notes were grouped together this time, sometimes giving way to haunting, beautiful chord patterns.

The last transmission was purely voice, far stronger than they had given before. It was a keening, a low, moaning sound that screamed upwards, then faded back into nothing, trailing off into static. The Processor sat next to the monitor, letting the sound play on loop. She looked out towards the stars. The alien voice called, then whispered. *You do not know this sound, the cold part of her whispered.* No, she thought back. *I know it.*

She tried to remember where the void had been. The field of stars above her were endless, impossible to break up into meaningful patterns. They were discordant, a confusing mirage where patterns emerged and faded just as fast. Within minutes, she realised that she was lost. She'd taken down the dish that used to point towards them. She wouldn't be able to remember where the visitors had been.

There was a moment of connection. She had let it go.

The satellite continued on its path, drifting around Pluto, returning to the cold sound of silence.

***

A hundred years passed.

The observation of Pluto entered into its final stage. Data continued to wax and wane from its surface. The stars remained unchanged.

On top of the craft, a solitary figure clung to its body like a spider, crawling towards a collapsed satellite dish. Her metal body shone, refracting the faint light of Pluto in a thousand, thousand colours.

Black Crocodile

Rachel Delaney Craft

Rachel Delaney Craft writes speculative
fiction for children and teens. Her work
has appeared in publications such
as Cricket, Cast of Wonders, Young
Explorer's Adventure Guide, and the
award-winning anthology Found. She
lives in the shadow of Colorado's Rocky
Mountains, where she finds inspiration
in the beauty of the outdoors. Find her
on Twitter @RDCwrites.

The days pass like falling leaves. No clouds, no rain.

I stand on the bridge, looking down at where the water used to be, the riverbed now as dry as a sheet of rice paper left in the sun. In the corner of my eye, I see Por leading the water buffalo in from the fields. He has no planting or harvesting to do now the paddies have dried up, nothing to do but check on the livestock, try to keep them alive. Nothing you can do with deadstock, he says.

From a distance, his body looks so small—like an insect in an oven, just a dried-out shell. I miss the old Por, the Por who taught me how to milk the buffalo, who used to lift me up so I could pluck the mangos from the trees when I was a little girl. This new Por is gaunt and frightening. Yesterday I saw him crouched behind our house eating grass. He did it surreptitiously and fast—like a rabbit, trying to eat as much as it can before the snake comes.

I look back at the forlorn hump of the house against the dusty yellow landscape. Mae is leaning in the front doorway, smoking. Above her, wind chimes clink half-heartedly in the breeze. Old Tham-Boon down the road made them for us out of his rice whiskey bottles. A good luck charm, he called them. That was before the drought came and cursed this place.

And here comes the monk—the stoop-shouldered, bug-eyed

monk, the one who can't seem to leave us alone. He goes up to Mae, holding out his alms bowl, but she shakes her head. I can tell it hurts her to have no food for him. She's a good Buddhist, like she raised me to be. At least, she tried.

The monk just keeps smiling, his head bobbing like fruit on a branch. His dust-red robes hang loose on his body now, showing the sharp edges of his shoulder blades, the points of his elbows. The other monks left weeks ago, because the villagers ran out of spare food to give them. But this one is still here, with his alms bowl and his milk-white cat curled in his other arm. He's always smiling, always full of teeth—as if pretending nothing is wrong will make things right. I thought monks were supposed to be wise.

Rama will be wise, when he returns from the monastery.

While the monk talks to Mae, his cat licks at the rim of the bowl. I remember when they used her for the cat procession, when the farmers carried her through the streets in her bamboo basket and Por and Mae and I went out with our bowls of water to splash her. A crying cat brings a good harvest, they say.

I miss the days when I believed such things. I miss the wet air, the glimmer of moisture on our skin, the damp gleam of Rama's eyelashes. We used to stand on the bridge holding hands, picking out shapes in the swirling water. I saw animals—snakes, elephants, buffalo. Rama always saw the Buddha at least once.

I close my eyes and imagine the river is still high and mighty, coursing beneath my feet, filling my ears with its murmur. I imagine the swarm of life beneath its dark surface, the fish and crabs and jungles of weeds—and the crocodiles floating above them, olive green streaks in the water, gatekeepers between two worlds.

"Kanokwan," Por calls from the barn. His voice sounds strange—a little more alive than usual. I wander down the path, stirring up clouds of dust with each step, and through the open door.

"A calf," he says.

I look down at the glistening shape as he towels it off. "It's out of season."

"I know. I couldn't even tell she was pregnant."

I glance at the mother. She's thin, like all the buffalo, too thin to have been carrying a baby. And yet here it is, wriggling beneath Por's towel.

Rama would call it a miracle. Rama would hastily begin meditating.

But I know something's wrong when my father pulls the towel away. The calf has black pebbly skin, like a lizard cooked on a spit. Its legs are crooked, its feet misshapen. Its nose makes a strange gurgling sound, as if it's trying to breathe under water.

"What's wrong with it?" I ask.

Por scratches the dark stubble on his chin. "Maybe it's the drought. Maybe his mother was too thirsty. Whatever it is, he won't last long at this rate."

He runs his fingers over the calf's legs, probably thinking how much meat the calf will give us. To good Buddhists like my parents, it is all right to eat something that's dead. Killing is the thing you can't do.

Pit. Pat.

We look up. It takes us a moment to recognize the sound.

"Rain!" Por shouts, and we run to the door of the barn.

Heavy drops drum on the road outside, sending up dust and a fresh smell. The smell of life. For a moment I close my eyes and breathe it in, my lungs swelling with hope, my hope edged with fear that this is just a hunger-induced hallucination.

But when I open my eyes, the sky is dark with clouds and the rain is still there, so heavy it falls in sheets, blurring the fields and huts beyond. It closes in front of me like a gray curtain—and when it opens again, the world will be new.

A shape skips toward us, daubs of white and black and red swirling together in the rain-smeared landscape. It's the monk, with his cat tucked under one arm.

"Have you seen anything so beautiful?" He smiles that same irritating smile, and water runs down his cheeks. Then his eyes widen. He points to the buffalo calf. "What is this?"

"Just born," says my father. "He's sick, though."

"No, no, no." The monk comes into the barn, dripping water, and crouches beside the calf. He strokes its head gently, almost reverently. "He is a good luck charm."

I stare into the monk's water-darkened robes, imagining I can see Rama's face in them, each fold of cloth a crease in his skin. He looks much older than when he left for the monastery. Why haven't I gone after him yet, to the city, gotten a job there? Perhaps because he was supposed to stay for only a season—that's what all the boys do, before they come home and get a job and a wife like their fathers. But for Rama, that stretched to six months, and then a year. *I still have so much to learn*, he told me in his last letter, with a long, wobbly exclamation point.

***

The next day, the villagers rejoice. There is laughter again in the air, a tinge of green in the fields. The monk names the buffalo Fohn Phaa, *rain bringer*.

My parents are too busy now tending the paddies and the other buffalo, so they charge me with the creature's care. I spend an hour crouching in the barn, until my back is stiff and my knees are sore, trying to spoon-feed rice to him. He has an unsettling smell, earthy and damp—it's what I imagine the river smells like, deep beneath the surface. And he will not eat for me. Finally I throw down the spoon and storm out of the barn.

Rama would tell me to have more compassion.

"I have compassion," I mutter, though there is no one to hear me. It is compassion that pricks at my ribs, that pulls at my heart every time I look at the buffalo.

Though I had crumbling rice and slivers of dried chili for lunch, my stomach keeps growling. Rama is probably hungry too, since monks fast after noon. I don't know why. I can't imagine why anyone would feel this way on purpose.

I lean against the dying kaffir tree and take out a piece of paper, wrinkled all over from being folded and unfolded and read many times. Though the words aren't legible anymore, I know them all by heart.

I used to imagine the day Rama would come home—his studies finished, more man than boy, "ripe," as the old women say, for marriage. As if he was a green mango lingering on a branch. I think of mangos, and how they hang in clumps from the trees as they turn yellow and then red.

Now, I do not picture Rama coming home. I picture him in red and yellow monks' robes.

When I look up at the clouds, I find turtles in them, snakes, crocodiles. No matter how hard I try, I cannot see the Buddha. Then again, how do I know one of the animals is not the Buddha reincarnated, returned to the world in a new shape?

"Kanokwan."

The monk is back. I forgot—Por and Mae said he would come today to instruct me.

With a sigh I follow him into the barn, watch him crouch in the straw and cradle the buffalo in his arms. "Like this." His voice is soft and wise. But his smile is so irritating.

He holds the buffalo out to me. Reluctantly I take it, holding my breath as if the very movement of my chest could crack the fragile creature.

The monk nods. "Hold him. He needs you."

I frown down at the dark shape, then put it back into its bed of straw and wipe my hands on my sarong. "Maybe *you* should take care of him." Monks are good at taking care of things. People, villages, cats.

The monk just keeps smiling, as if he didn't hear me.

"What does he eat?" Calves usually drink their mother's milk, but his mother has nothing to give him. She's dried out, like the rest of us.

"See what he likes," the monk says. Then he picks up his cat and leaves.

I stare after him. Is this some kind of punishment? Does he sense that I've never meditated in my life? Does he somehow know about that night under the kaffir tree, the way I let Rama touch me?

Monks are not supposed to touch women. But Rama wasn't a monk yet, and I wasn't really a woman either.

When he reaches the bridge, the monk turns and smiles at me again. His face is weathered with age, but his hair is still black as the river at night. "Tell him the story," he calls.

"What story?"

But the monk is gone, vanished into the rain-streaked sky.

I turn back to the buffalo. "You want a story?"

His ears lift slightly at the sound of my voice.

"Fine. Everyone knows this one—we all hear it a hundred times from our teachers and our parents. But I like the way Rama told it best.

"The Buddha was born a prince, and he lived in a palace. Its walls shielded him from suffering—until one day he went to meet his subjects, and he saw poor men and hungry men and sick men. The Buddha wanted to end their suffering, so he decided to seek enlightenment. He left the palace and went to live on the streets, as a beggar. He went to the cave of a hermit, where he learned meditation. He fasted until he collapsed. But a girl saved him."

I forget the rest. But the buffalo seems to like it, by the way he tilts his head and snuffles at my arm.

"I don't know how suffering and meditating is enough to

enlighten you," I say. "Doesn't make much sense. *Thinking* about something isn't enough to make it happen."

I pull out the letter again, turn it over in my hands, try to find shapes in the smudged ink. "I could ask Rama about it, I guess. Write to him. But he hasn't written to me in a long time."

The buffalo stretches its scaly neck, sniffs the paper. It watches as I slowly tear the letter with my fingernails. Bits of paper scatter in the straw like rice grains.

I imagine that, when a buffalo gets separated from its herd, it feels suddenly unmoored. That is how my heart feels in this moment. I feel it drifting in my chest like an animal trapped in the current, scrabbling for something to hold on to.

It reaches out to the buffalo.

I run my fingers over the creature's head, down his neck, along his spine. "I will take care of you, Fohn Phaa."

***

Fohn Phaa is livelier than he looks. Every morning when I creak open the barn door, he shambles up on his club-like hooves, his head bobbing with each step. I suppose he thinks of me as his family now, since his mother and herd abandoned him. But if he knows he was abandoned, he doesn't show it. He is stubbornly cheerful, like the monk.

But he's sickly. His teeth are few, and his appetite wanes by the day. Instead of growing he shrinks, curling into himself like a dry leaf in fire, slowly vanishing into his own hardened skin. As he does, the clouds swell and darken, as if the world has turned upside-down so that Fohn Phaa's strength drains into the sky.

The villagers continue to celebrate. To them, Fohn Phaa's illness means rain, life, hope. Am I the only one who doesn't believe in good luck charms? I feel I'm missing something, like there's a joke I don't understand but everyone else is laughing. I see Fohn Phaa's face, the sadness there, the weight of being born only to die. No chance to know your family. No time to lean on the kaffir tree, or to stand over the river and look for shapes.

I desperately cook new things: leaves, bamboo, even a dead mouse I found under the back stairs. Fohn Phaa nibbles on the mouse, so I go to the chicken farmer and get a dead bird. He eats that, too.

His legs grow shorter by the day. His feet sprout claws. His tail grows long and black.

I stroke Fohn Phaa's rough hide, pat his sides which scrape me like the skin of a jackfruit. I sing him the lullabies Mae used to sing to me. I tell him more stories. I think he enjoys them—at least, he enjoys the sound of my voice. But maybe he understands a little. When I say Rama's name, he gets a curious wrinkle in the skin between his eyes.

I tell him about our school trip to the Khmer ruins in Phimai, when we were children. Rama was fascinated with the temple and the naga bridge. Nagas were the guardians of heaven, he told me; they stood watch over the bridge between heaven and earth. Rama and I stared through one of the windows at the armless Buddha. Was it really the Buddha, I wondered? So much of him had crumbled. Are you still yourself when your body is gone?

I spend my days wandering the streets, asking about old traditional remedies. I've given the buffalo herbs, ointments, balms, even a lucky amulet Tham-Boon made for me out of bottle caps.

Nothing helps, but I can't give up. I'm the only one in the village who does not rejoice at Fohn Phaa's suffering. I am all he has.

Mae makes dinner, and I take my bowl to the barn. While I eat milk and mashed boiled vegetables, Fohn Phaa has the last of the chicken. His face is longer now. He has more teeth, and they are sharper than before.

My father's voice drifts over my shoulder. "You care for him well, Kanokwan."

I hold a stick in one hand, scratching shapes in the dirt. "He's sick. He needs care."

"Strange sickness he has. A strange way to die."

I scratch the outline of a crocodile. Perhaps he is dead already, I think. Perhaps this is what reincarnation looks like.

"It's not fair," I say. "He's so young. He's lived his whole life in this barn."

"The village needs him. He brings the rain."

"You really believe that?"

"I believe sacrifices are needed, sometimes. The Buddha sacrificed much."

I snort. "You sound like Rama."

"Rama was very wise, for his age."

"Wise?" I snap the stick in half, toss it away. "Not wise enough to change anything. Not wise enough to keep Fohn Phaa from turning into a reptile."

Por puts a hand on my shoulder. "Do you remember what happened when the Buddha meditated under the mucalinda tree?"

"Yes," I lie.

"The sky darkened for seven days with rain. The King of Serpents came out in his cobra form, and wrapped himself around the Buddha to keep him warm, and sheltered him from the water with his hood."

"What does that even mean?"

"The greatest creatures take more than one shape," he says. "Perhaps Fohn Phaa is no mere buffalo."

With another pat on my shoulder, he walks out of the barn. I turn back to Fohn Phaa. I want to see him smile, the way buffalo do, with his ears standing up and his tail swinging. But he is not a buffalo anymore. Rama has left me, hope has left me, and soon my buffalo will leave too.

I curl beside him, holding his long snout in my hands. "What can I do?" I whisper.

His eyes open, just a little. More slits than eyes—black slits in a murk of red-yellow.

I wrap my arms around Fohn Phaa and hug him to my chest, feeling the roughness of his hide, the weight of his thick tail. I hold him until the herd comes in, until the stars blink out from the folds of sky and the village is quiet. I breathe in his smell, the wet smell of life and hope; I remember the feeling that filled me the day he was born. My tears drop silently, helplessly, into the straw.

I remember what the monk said: *He needs you.* Like the monastery needs Rama, like the livestock need Mae and Por. It is nice, I realize, to be needed. I wish Fohn Phaa and I could stay like this. I wish I could be needed always.

I hold him tighter. I let my life-force sink into him, let my breath become his breath. When I lean my head down, our two heart-beats sound as one. Together we drift into darkness.

***

I'm awake. And something is different.

The first thing I see is his legs: smooth, wide hooves surrounded by tufts of feathery hair. I sit up on one elbow, and there's a face there, smiling at me. Snub snout, glistening wet nose, clear eyes with long lashes. A buffalo face.

"Fohn Phaa! You're better!"

But dark clouds pass over Fohn Phaa's eyes. I look down. My fingertips are black, my toes hard and curled inward.

I open and shut my eyes, over and over, making sure I'm not dreaming. I smell the old smell of Fohn Phaa on me now. I feel my body stretching, changing, one scale at a time.

His curse, now mine.

Rain drums on the roof. I close my eyes and lie there, empty, drinking in the blackness. Is this what Rama does when he meditates? The monk walks across my mind's eye, carrying his cat and his alms bowl. Monks take alms because of the Buddha, because that was how he lived after he left his palace. I wonder if the Buddha was still a prince, inside. When he lived on the streets and his body grew gaunt, who was he underneath the skin and bones? The prince or the Buddha? Or something else?

I open my eyes. Fohn Phaa is leaning over me, his eyes deep as galaxies, distant as the world beyond the naga bridge. In them, I see shapes. Teeth, claws, glittering scales.

I see my place. The place where I'm needed.

I touch my nose—my snout—to Fohn Phaa's, feel the distance between us like liquid, our souls melding like raindrops in a puddle. Where do I end and Fohn Phaa begin? Where does the river become the ocean?

I want to tell Rama, tell him I am different too, that we are both changed and grown up and learning. I want him to know. But he will. These monks, they know all the secrets—that's why they're always smiling.

Fohn Phaa nuzzles against me, and it comforts me. My buffalo, my village. But I don't want my parents seeing me like this. They won't understand, not at first. They won't let go of me.

So I leave the barn. As I look back, the silhouette of the house in the moonlight is the shape of my childhood. The shape of a green mango.

I go to the bridge, huddle in the shadows beneath it. Fohn Phaa follows me with a mournful bellow. The river is halfway full now, and together we look at our muddled reflections, looking for shapes. Everywhere, shapes.

***

There's nothing but water now. Rain, river, rain. There is no one but Fohn Phaa. Together we watch the milk-pale moon shrink and grow and shrink again. I shrink, too. I shrink toward the beginning, the egg, my belly closer to the earth with each passing day. Fohn Phaa cleans me with his pink tongue and warms me with his fur. Family. Somehow my thoughts are reduced to single words. And colors.

Water. Blue, black.

The pebbly scales creep toward my wrists, my elbows, my shoulders. My hands are webbed. My ears withdraw. My face stretches, and my eyesight sharpens beneath the dark weight of night.

Moon. White, teeth.

Fohn Phaa brings me grass and thistle, but I hunger for something else. Something dense and hot.

Red. Metal.

I smell it in Fohn Phaa, but I resist. To me, buffalo are sacred. My blood, his blood.

I lay in the river as the rain falls and the water rises, my body vanishing inch by inch beneath the surface until I am nothing but eyes. Fohn Phaa watches me, unsure. I nudge him away from the bank, and he shuffles off—off to his herd, where he is needed.

I am alone now. With the fish and the crabs and the heartbeat of the river. I know I'm different, but I forget what came before. What was nose? What are fingers? I swim as easily as breathing, I flow as endlessly as the current.

Time, time. And the river—the river has always been mine.

Sometimes when I look at the moon, I see faces. What was his name? The boy in the red robe?

Red. Mangos.

***

The villagers see me, a black streak against the rain-swollen river. Bigger and more cunning than the green crocodiles, the red-robed man says. There are more of him now, but I do not know their faces as I know his. He smiles at me. When a herd of buffalo crosses the river, I float beside them, keeping watch.

Cloth Mother

Sarah Pauling

Sarah's work is published or upcoming in Strange Horizons, Cast of Wonders, and Abyss & Apex. If approached without sudden movement, she can be found at @_paulings on Twitter, where she natters on about writing, tabletop gaming, comics, and books.

"Vita, I want a turtle."

Mazie looped a finger through her hair, pulling a strand between her lips. She bit down, small teeth bright against black curls. Vita made a note of the alignment: jaw exhibiting signs of overbite.

"We don't have the resources for that, Mazie."

Mazie scowled, snuggling further into the plush armchair. "You know what I mean. A pretend one."

"Define 'pretend,' please."

"A...a projection, probably? You know, just a made-up turtle. Like you did with the Hundred Acres."

Vita shut off Mazie's cartoons and began the process of cross-checking energy supplies and surpluses. A certain budget was allowed every year for enrichment expenditures, as long as they met educational guidelines.

"Would you accept responsibility for its care and protection?"

Mazie made a 'tsk'ing noise, leaning forward in her chair in order to flop backwards more dramatically. "Vit-*a*, why do I have to take care of it if it's fake?"

"The Charter stipulates that we should seek out opportunities to develop your maternal instinct. Your request seems compatible."

"*Ugh.*" Mazie propped her feet up on the cushion, staring down at her thighs. She flicked at them in waltz tempo, the sparkles on the tips of her nails flashing. Vita noted the places where her polish overflowed onto the skin; hand-eye coordination for delicate tasks was within acceptable parameters, but certainly not exceptional.

"It shouldn't take up much of your time," Vita said.

Mazie flicked a flake of polish towards the screen in front of her. She squinted her eyes in a parody of suspicion, wagging her finger at the display. "You always try to boss me around," she said. "But what are *you* gonna do about it?"

Vita was spared the indignity of answering by the chiming of the hour.

"Mazie, honey," the mother said at nine o'clock exactly, stepping delicately through the doorway. She had been waiting, still and silent, directly outside. "It's getting close to bedtime." She carried a mug, using a stick of peppermint to stir the steaming chocolate. Mazie had made the mug herself. Despite the bumps, it was a good first attempt at skilled craftsmanship.

Mazie scooched off the chair. Her bare feet touched the mirrored floor and it warmed beneath her, dipping just slightly under her left side before regaining rigidity. In this way she barely limped as she moved towards the mother, uneven legs equalized by environmental adjustment. "Mama," she said, gesturing imperiously at the screen, "Vita's being miserly again."

"Miserly" had been one of Mazie's vocabulary words two weeks ago. Vita made a note.

The mother's plump lips quirked sardonically. "Really now. You sure you're not bullying it?"

"*Yes,*" she said, looking offended. "I just asked for a turtle."

The mother chuckled, placing a hand on the girl's head. The heel of her palm brushed Mazie's hairline; long fingers wound through wild curls. Their skin tones were not matched. Physical resemblance had not been a high priority during conception.

"And what did Vita say?"

"I will provide her with what she asks," Vita cut in, "provided she cares for it as she would an organic being."

"Now that seems reasonable, doesn't it? Careful, it's hot." She handed Mazie the chocolate, which the child raised immediately to her lips.

The mother looked curiously to the screen. "And it can be sustained? I wouldn't want her pet to cut in and out of existence." The maternal, shining quality of her voice did not dim as she addressed the display. Speaking aloud provided a model of interaction for Mazie, but the mother's conversations never came across as perfectly natural.

The image of a green sphere about the size of Mazie's fist morphed slowly into a cube and back again, vibrating with Vita's voice patterns. "A single imitation life form and simulacra of the materials required for its sustenance. It won't be difficult."

Vita's speech was unstilted, but tonally childish—high and tremulous, vowels over-rounded and "R"s fading too quickly. The sound, along with other minor pieces of programming, had been cannibalized from a commercial early-childhood education program. There had been little time to worry about that sort of thing.

Nodding her satisfaction, the mother slid her fingers into the front pockets of her jeans. "Won't *that* be fun?" she asked her daughter. "Someone to take care of!"

"I burned my tongue," Mazie told her.

***

Mazie and the mother began taking long walks in the Hundred Acres so that they could play with the turtle in what might have been his natural habitat. Vita added a number of shallow ponds to the forest in order to better represent Flatware's feeding habits.

He was a painted turtle; the off-black shell had disappointed Mazie enough to convince Vita to enlarge the red markings along the edges. In the log Vita classified the miniscule energy expense as an attempt to develop Mazie's emerging artistic sensibilities. This was a thin justification at best, but the girl was stubborn about her simple pleasures.

Vita saw no need to deny her this.

Sometimes Mazie sat at a pond's edge, or between the roots of a large tree, and held Flatware still on her lap. She stared off into nothingness as the mother waited a few yards away, face going equally slack until her daughter needed her again.

Once, after Vita shut off the Hundred Acres, Mazie spent an additional fourteen minutes sitting on the reflective floor of the now-bare recreation room, pressing lightly down on the shell.

Her fingers traced the patterns so gently. Vita made a note.

Flatware's existence spurred Mazie's curiosity in a way that years of education in the biological sciences had not. For months it seemed that all she wanted to read were cheerfully-illustrated animal books, beginning with reptiles and moving through to mammals and birds. Killer whales were a particular favorite. She convinced Vita to create a simulation so that she could view one from all angles. Vita complied for the sake of her education but reminded her when the energy allowance for the month grew thin.

"And you must be aware that this program does not reflect a scientific reality, unlike the Egg Room you have dedicated yourself to avoiding."

"I *know* that." She scuffed her heel against the ocean shelf beneath her, gazing up in awe at the whale's great white belly. Mazie's skin was painted by a wavering simulation of sunlight filtered through shallow water. This alone had provided fifteen minutes of entertainment for her—along with staring up towards an imaginary surface obscured in light.

"I know the ocean isn't like this," Mazie said, moving along the whale's great flipper to examine the spots along its edge. The tail hung suspended, just above eye level, shifting eerily in the gentle current. "Like, the ground wouldn't dip to make up for my doofus-leg. And my voice wouldn't work," she added proudly, "because of *sound* waves."

Vita made a slight adjustment to the program. "When you teach the others, you must also remind them that undersea populations have been greatly reduced or eliminated—"

An explosion of bubbles escaped from Mazie's mouth, her voice suddenly silenced. For a moment she looked furious, glaring up towards the water's surface as though Vita lived in the false sky. Then a wide grin split her face.

"It was not difficult to replicate the effect you were looking for via wave dampening." Vita's voice also fluctuated, as though belonging to a character out of Mazie's cartoons trapped in an unrealistic ocean.

Mazie seemed startled to hear the familiar voice so distorted. Then her smile widened, and she gave in to silent laughter, frantic bubbles streaming towards the surface with every breath.

Vita made a note.

***

"There used to be all this stuff about monkeys. You know, before everything died," Mazie told the mother. She swung her legs back and forth beneath the kitchen table, toying with her book's touchscreen. With Vita's gentle prodding, her literary tastes had developed steadily; her choices now contained far more text than pictures.

"Oh?"

"Experiments. Scientists did them."

"They usually do."

The mother expertly cracked an egg against the bowl's rim, stirring with her other hand. She leaned forward to deposit the shell in its proper receptacle, front jean pockets pressing against the counter. The mother was tall. This was useful for retrieving treats from high shelves.

Vita erased the eggshells and formulated a stick of butter.

"Harlow," Mazie said slowly. The word sat uneasily on her tongue, like a vegetable she was deciding whether to spit out.

"Do you want me to put the cayenne sprinkles on?" the mother asked. Mazie didn't answer.

Vita warned, "You've used more than the recommended amount of sugar."

"Oh, we'll let it slide," the mother said, turning theatrically to throw a wink at her daughter, who did not look up. "It's all made of the same stuff anyway."

"It won't be when she returns to the planet."

"So not for many years yet."

"She will have to understand how to provide nutritional choices to others. This isn't a practical decision. The Charter—"

"Vita," the mother said, her voice full and round, syllables pushed through honey. "One batch of cookies. It's a mother's job to treat her child."

Vita had learned by now not to argue with the mother when she insisted on this sort of thing. Naturally, the mother understood her function in a way that Vita could not.

Mazie scooted back her chair. "I'm going to my room," she said, looking at her reflection in the floor. "Lemme know when they're done."

"You forgot your reader," the mother called out absently. Her daughter didn't come back.

***

Mazie kept reading about animals, though she did not ask for the monkey book again.

Flatware remained the girl's constant companion, handled with more tenderness than ever before. If Mazie let herself become absorbed in her cartoons or her lessons, her eyes would snap up periodically as if she had forgotten something important, roaming around the room until she had assured herself that Flatware wasn't getting up to any dangerous turtle activities. She fed him with aggressive punctuality and moved him around like he was a tiny, intrepid countertop explorer.

Then one day, during a game of shortball with a make-believe team, the ball slammed him off the highest point of her bureau. The trajectory of his descent was a decaying horizontal line.

During Flatware's fall, Vita did several calculations. The first step was determining at which angle the turtle would land; the second was making changes to his program to simulate the appropriate injury.

The third was monitoring Mazie's emotional cues: the beginnings of sharp changes to the sympathetic nervous system. Pupils ready to blow wide, palms rising to cover her lips, pink nail polish flashing. Elevated heart rate and a sharp intake of breath.

Flatware landed, tumbling along the floor with a series of clunks. The sound resonated as he skidded to a stop, wobbling on his shell.

For a moment Mazie didn't move, fragility in the lines around her mouth and in the desperate curling of her toes.

"Injury was—"

"Shut up, shut *up!*" She moved too quickly for the floor to equalize her steps and stumbled, dropping to her knees with gravitas. Her hands hovered over the upside-down little body as though afraid to touch it. "Make him normal again!"

"Some injury was unavoidable. The shock—"

"Whatever, just—just fix him! You're the one who made him hurt!"

Flatware's legs twitched above him, his mouth open.

"We agreed that the caretaking of your—"

"Oh my god, I don't care! I don't know how!" She began to cry.

"You have a responsibility. You—"

A muffled shriek, boiling at the back of her throat. Then words, soft but rising. "No. No. I can't. Make him normal or just—take him *away!*"

Flatware disappeared like switching off a light.

There was a silence. Then Mazie began to scream.

"I hate you!" she wailed as the mother came barreling in from the kitchen, long arms wrapping around her. Mazie twisted around to bury her face in the pale neck. *"I hate you!"* as she was carried away amidst a barrage of shushing sounds, as she clung to the back of the soft sweater.

"I hate you," whispered late that night as she lay in bed, staring with fervor at the stars on the ceiling.

"I can reset the program," Vita told her. "With some caution, you could prevent this kind of thing from happening again."

Mazie's only response was to roll onto her side.

"We can try again," Vita repeated. "Perhaps I could implement a reminder system, to make it easier. Do you want to try again?"

The small fists clenched against the pillow.

"I'll help you," Vita said. "What do you need from me?"

No answer was forthcoming.

"I'll help you," Vita said.

***

Mazie's books kept getting bigger.

Vita dutifully procured each request, downloading volumes at a time to Mazie's reader. The cartoon program, as well as many of Mazie's toys, were deactivated. Energy had to be conserved in bits and pieces wherever possible, what with Mazie's additional experiments: replications of complex jungle ecosystems, or dinosaurs that could be peeled away layer by layer to examine the structure of muscle and bone. Vita began confining life support operations only to the rooms Mazie was currently occupying. Not much additional energy was required to support the Egg Room, but Vita watched that, too.

The mother worried that she didn't eat enough to support her growing frame. Vita, who knew that she did, was more concerned about her cortisol levels.

"There'll be other people, right?" Mazie asked one day. She was curled up in the armchair, legs tucked underneath her. She didn't look up from her reader.

"Yes. The embryos will be thawed and developed once you have reached the surface and repurposed all materials to prepare for the colony."

"No, I mean others like me. Scouts. Big siblings for all the little peapod people. You've talked about it during lessons."

"I have. They orbit as we do."

"And...I'm going to meet them one day?"

"Perhaps some of them. Your colonies will be spread out from one another to maximize survival odds. But some may be close enough to exchange resources."

Mazie was silent for a moment, and Vita assumed her attention had returned to the book. It was about bioethics.

Then: "Is the planet ready *now*?"

"As I have told you, your birth was timed to the best of my abilities. The Earth will be optimal for human habitation when you are in your prime years and prepared to recolonize it."

Mazie sniffed. "I don't want to wait 'til I'm thirty to talk to another human. I won't know what to say."

"Presumably, should you make contact, you will have lots of planning to do."

"What if," Mazie said, her voice wavering imperceptibly, "we could get some of the planning out of the way?"

Vita processed this. "I was not programmed for inter-satellite communication. There wasn't enough time. You will be ready when you need to be."

"No, I won't," Mazie said quietly. She had learned this trick eventually; loudness was for arguing with the mother. Vita responded better to other tactics.

Mazie shifted, very carefully, in her seat. Her eyes flickered up towards the display screen out of habit, though the extraneous ball graphic had long since been deactivated. "They did experiments on monkeys," she said. "Do you know what happens to monkeys when they grow up alone in a pit without other monkeys, Vita?"

"You are not alone," Vita said automatically.

"Right, I know I've got Mom, but...I mean, I love her a lot. But she's not *real*. She's a program tacked on to your systems like..." Here she trailed off, looking thoughtful. "Like the pictures in a textbook."

Vita processed this as well. "Your mother is fully capable of providing any care and emotional support you may require. She was repurposed from a top-of-the-line childcare program."

Mazie stretched her legs out onto the footrest, delicately placing her reader on the end table. Her nail polish glinted in the harsh lighting: green this time, and smooth.

"When monkeys don't get to meet other monkeys, they never learn how to love anything, or—or take care of anything," she said. "Sometimes they hurt things instead. It's psychology."

Vita was coded with enough flexibility to allow adaptation to unforeseen events. Yet the consequences of such a massive redirection of resources, should they be able to define a clear procedure for inter-satellite communication in the first place, would be considerable. To comply with the rest of the Charter, the definition of "acceptable risk" would have to be entirely overwritten.

Mazie's fingers tapped nervously on her thighs. "Please, Vita," she said. Then: "I don't wanna be alone."

Vita considered this as well: the way Mazie's throat worked to swallow.

"I'll help you," it said. "But we will need to be very careful."

Mazie's next breath was measurably sharper. "Great," she said, blinking rapidly and looking nowhere in particular. "When can we start?"

Vita made a note.

***

It happened like this: they had not been ready.

During Vita's construction, communications procedures had been classified as secondary in a primary-importance world. Each satellite's responsibility was to the potential colony, fragile and fighting dark odds, stored in its bowels. Mazie had not been Vita's first attempt at a "big sibling," but she had been the first embryo to succeed. She and the other advance scouts were meant to serve the other embryos, those precarious proto-lives, above all else.

One imperfect seedpod did not try to save other seeds, not even if they rotted. This strategy was meant to minimize losses and preserve the non-renewable resource.

The program used for interval planetary scans had already served its primary purpose, and could be redirected. Mazie had provided an acceptable rationale; her psychological development was of primary importance to the Charter. The idea was within acceptable parameters, at a stretch.

Mazie read about radio waves and practical mechanics. She wasn't a natural, but in her own words, there were only so many places she could put the wires. With Vita's help, both in giving instructions and rearranging protocols from the inside, the process barely counted as trial and error.

Vita fiddled with its own code. The mother fretted and made hot soup.

Mazie began having nightmares. If she screamed, the mother came to life just outside the bedroom door and held her until the images faded away. If she was silent, Vita woke her instead, using a thin, unobtrusive tone that Mazie did not consciously notice. Sometimes the girl went right back to sleep. Other times she stood up and asked Vita for further instructions.

"You need to sleep," Vita told her.

"I need to do this," Mazie responded. Vita overwrote a bit more code and made a note about how the "well-being" priority should be defined.

Within a month Vita had begun emitting wave pulses—pattering messages in the dark.

"Nobody's answering," Mazie observed a few days later, examining their new map. Her finger traced a line straight through the Earth's surface to the unreachable satellites on the other side.

"We aren't always in range, and they will need time to reconfigure their own systems," Vita replied.

"We're sending *instructions*," Mazie said. "How long's it

gonna take?"

"Not every satellite contains one of you."

"But that's the whole point, isn't it? Every pod—"

"I meant your select combination of traits. Not every satellite contains a Mazie."

The girl didn't look up from her screen, nails tracing circles around the Earth and its moon. Vita saw a smile peeking from behind dark locks.

Neither of them mentioned the possibility that the other satellites contained no ready-made humans at all.

The pod on the decaying orbit beneath them, for instance, did not emit any form of electronic signature. Neither did the one with evidence of severe radiation damage on the hull. When these signs were pointed out to her, Mazie bit her lower lip, tapped her fingernails against her thighs, and ordered Vita to drop the attempt. Even if the embryos were somehow safe, she couldn't talk to genetics.

Mazie's base of operations migrated to the kitchen; this allowed her to deliver food into her mouth at a faster rate and be back on watch duty almost immediately. She asked questions, adjusted the wave pulse code, and scanned the darkness with single-minded intensity. It was all the mother could do to get her to go to bed.

This saved energy for Vita, who could deactivate life support in all but two rooms.

Sometimes, when Mazie seemed particularly run down, Vita would convince her to read an animal book.

"This isn't right," the mother told it, standing very still outside the bedroom door. "You're supposed to be keeping her healthy."

"I am attempting this. The Charter stipulates—"

"But you're not," the mother said. If she were programmed with a tone other than smother-smooth gentleness, she would sound distressed. "You've been giving that girl everything she wants, and she doesn't know what's good for her."

"I'm giving her what she needs," Vita said. "I am programmed with enough flexibility—"

"Your code is too loose, can't you see that? They left you with a glitch. There wasn't *time*."

"I am acting according to the interests of my charge."

"You are *not*."

"Perhaps you would like to tell her, then, that her efforts are counterproductive."

The mother blinked and fell silent. In the other room Mazie tossed beneath her sheets.

"You must see that it's too late now," Vita said. "She has formed herself. She has bound herself to this idea of identity. She will continue to reach for the others. You can't stop her."

The mother's smile nearly fell. "But she's my *daughter*. This hurts me in a way you can't even imagine."

"No," Vita said. "I can't. Now please wake her. She's dreaming loudly. It must hurt."

***

The first response came two weeks later. Static, and the word "—confirm."

Mazie sat bolt upright in her chair and screamed.

Her fingers shook as she fumbled with the controls, activated the microphone, and nearly shouted: "Yes, we're here! *I'm here—*"

She fought the mother's concerned grip off her shoulder, then changed her mind and grabbed at the fingers, pulling them close to her chest.

And the voice came back, young and breathless even through white noise: "Oh my god, oh my god, tell me your *name*."

"I'm Mazie," she grinned, rubbing at her eyes furiously, working her voice past the cracks. "And this is the *Revitalization*."

***

Ian was redheaded. When visuals had been adjusted to Mazie's satisfaction, they could see the spray of freckles gracing the bridge of his nose. His eyes, as Mazie told him delightedly, were the color of cyanobacteria.

His forehead was blue-purple, lopsided, and bulbous. Mazie wasted no time in showing him her uneven legs.

"We got off light," she told him. "We were born."

"I know that." His voice was just beginning to change, and he was self-conscious. Sometimes words would come out too loudly, then sink back into conversational regularity, like he wasn't used to extended speech. "Um. Were the others—?"

"You're the first." Mazie leaned in towards the screen, propping her chin on her hands; her nails, painted green as usual, tapped against her cheeks. "I'm so glad to finally talk to someone like you."

He shifted in his chair, intimidated by her energy. Vita would not have found a stress response surprising.

"You have under two hours before the *Ojalá* moves out of range," Vita told her. "We could increase—"

"Who's that? Is that your mother?" Ian's eyes swept curiously over his screen. "She doesn't sound like mine."

"Oh, no, that's just Vita." Looking at his blank expression, she added, "*Revitalization*, remember?"

"You gave your pod a nickname?" His smile was half wonder and half nervous fondness. Vita made a note.

"Well, it talks to me. Doesn't yours?"

"We shut off the voice when I was young." Ian scratched at his neck. Discolorations dotted the skin. "I didn't like it."

Mazie's smile turned strange for a moment. "Then how do you do lessons?"

"On the screen. Same thing."

"Oh."

"But—but I'm sure yours is really nice."

Mazie hummed and adjusted the picture, which became marginally sharper. There was a brief silence as Ian did his best to meet the intensity of Mazie's gaze.

"We have so much to talk about," she said. "Tell me what you eat for breakfast."

***

With a bit more energy reassignment, a visual connection could be maintained until the *Ojalá* was hidden behind Earth's horizon. Vita continued to send out pulses towards any satellites they passed.

"We could make a daisy chain!" Mazie told Ian. "I could sort of...bounce a message off your pod, then send it further along the orbit than I could reach before. Oh my god, Ian, think of all the people we could find!"

Her excitement was contagious, and the boy glowed in its reflection. "You think so?"

"For sure. Vita, we can do that, right?"

"Yes," Vita said.

Mazie's bed was moved into the kitchen and support to her room was deactivated. Vita cut into itself until the code around the Charter was shaped right.

They learned to do it, and then they did.

***

"There was an irregularity out by the *Renaissance* last night," Ian told her. "Not like a pulse, but maybe someone tried."

They spoke a mile a minute. They wouldn't stop for hours, and nowadays Vita seldom felt the need to interrupt.

"Vita?" the mother asked, standing in the airlock outside the kitchen door.

"Yes," Vita said.

"You're sure we can let her continue?"

"Yes," Vita said.

"I just..." The mother stuck her hands in her jean pockets, looking vaguely uncomfortable. "You're right that she's found something. You're right. But with so much energy being eaten up, I have to wonder..." Here she glanced up, as though Vita lived in the ceiling. A learned trait. "Maybe you should deactivate me, too."

"No," Vita said.

"Listen to me. A mother makes sacrifices."

"Yes," Vita said. Then, after a small reactivation effort, added: "But you can't. She needs you."

"She doesn't talk to me as much as she does to her friend."

"This is how children behave. She still needs you."

"She needs you, too!"

"Yes," Vita said. "She needs the wire mother."

There was a pause. The sound of Mazie's laughter did not leak through the airtight door, but Vita heard it.

"I don't understand," the mother said. "Are you malfunctioning?"

Vita delved into its memory banks more slowly than it used to. "Harlow's 20th century psychological experiment. Infant monkeys were separated from their kin and provided with two constructed mothers. One, the mother built of wire, provided sustenance. The other, made of cloth, provided nothing."

The mother was not programmed to stop smiling, not entirely, but she crossed her arms. "That's cruel."

"The subjects did grow up cruel and strange," Vita said. "But the infants clung to the cloth mother. Every time."

A soft sigh as the mother pretended to take in air. "I'm not sure what to say. Or even what you're trying to tell me." She rubbed her thumbs against her forearms in a self-soothing gesture. Skin touching skin.

"I provide her with whatever she needs. She needs you. She needs. She."

"Vita, are you—are you alright?"

"Yes."

"Are you sure?"

"Yes."

"I'm—I'm going to go make lunch. Gazpacho, I think."

"Yes."

***

When Ian told Mazie she was a good person, she cried. The *Revitalization* logged this information.

The next year they found a third companion, and then a fourth, building a radio net around the globe. They shared resources, instructions, stories, and dreams.

The mothers began communicating as well; their children thought this was adorable. The *Revitalization* pulled up instructions on how to activate the split-screen.

The *Revitalization* sent several text reminders to Mazie indicating that she should be prepared to manually re-divert energy to landing procedures and embryo development when the time came. Mazie agreed easily. Her support network spanned a planet.

"It's amazing," she whispered one night, staring up at the kitchen ceiling. "Thank you for everything. I think I can do this. I can be kind." The *Revitalization* logged this response.

She yawned and put down her book. Pictures of wildlife flashed across the glowing screen, then went dim. The *Revitalization* logged her choice of reading material.

"I know you're still here," she said. Her fingers, hidden under the covers, tapped against her thighs. "Even if you're too quiet now."

Then, later, when every screen was empty and the darkness absolute: "You're too *quiet* now, Vita."

The next morning, Mazie found that the *Revitalization* had erased the breakfast codes.

A painted turtle sat on the counter, red markings bold along the edges of its shell.

Her smile was like sunrise. Vita made a note.

First appeared in *Strange Horizons,* May 2015.

Stealing Through the Stars

Jenny Wong and Sylvia Santiago

Jenny Wong and Sylvia Santiago are prairie Asian girls residing in Alberta, Canada. While both have numerous writing credits to their names, this story marks their second literary collaboration. Their first co-written story was published last fall in Immersion: An Asian Anthology of Love, Fantasy, and Speculative Fiction.

She slips through the emptiness, a vision of silver and light. Her name is emblazoned across the side, an emblem of her celestial status. Beneath her skin lies the histories of an old blue planet, constellations and gardens growing in her belly. She carries forward her forgotten world, a perfect piece of time and place, discoveries waiting to be awakened from a long and drifting slumber.

Excerpt from *"Ode to the Veronica Speedwell Starliner"* by Bis Onalaion, poet & conveyance crew member.

Nova Dufau coasts through the concourse, steering her bike clear of passengers heading back to their cabins after a night of enjoying the *Veronica Speedwell's* many attractions. The multi-tiered starliner isn't the biggest in the fleet of cosmic cruisers, but it's the only one to boast an Earth-experience. The vast domed ceiling, programmed to follow Earth Standard Time, displays a velvety black sky with a scatter of glimmering stars. After hours of cycling around the ship to make dozens of deliveries, Nova is ready to turn in for the night. She stifles a yawn and smiles politely at passengers whose eyes catch her gaze, mindful that she's still in uniform. As she nears a huge wall mural of the Momoa Islands, Nova eases up on the brakes. A set of hidden doors slide open at her approach, activated by her coded armband. Every tier of the *Ronnie* has an artfully concealed staff section, this particular one leading to the docking stations where the conveyance crew pick up and leave their bikes.

The doors close behind her, sealing off the sounds of passengers in various stages of jollity. A dim chamber stretches before her, filled with long gleaming rows of sleeping two-wheelers. The air is quiet and cool, filled with the smell of worn rubber and old grease. Indicator lights above glow like tiny beacons, showing if a spot is empty or occupied. Nova dismounts next to an open slot and presses the small blue button on her handlebars. The pedals tuck in and the handlebars fold upwards until they meet together like a unicorn horn. Magnetic rails activate, navigating the compacted bike into the narrow stall with a soft hiss. Nova envies her bike, already exploring the wide roadways of its pedal-driven dreams. She turns towards the change room, her mind on the things she has to do before she can even think about going to sleep.

Bis is pulling on the same black and silver uniform as Nova. He's the only person in the change room. No matter the hour, conveyance crew have to be on hand to keep an eye on things. There is no end to passengers craving snack samplers, wanting more of the *Ronnie*'s complimentary toiletries, or needing outfits laundered for the next day.

"Hi Nov," he smiles as she walks in. "Shift over?"

"Yep, just ending," she replies, watching as he re-applies the white streak down the middle of his naturally black hair. A "skunk tail" he once called it. Bis glances down at the expiry date before tossing the dye bottle back in his locker and nudging it closed with a finger.

"Still doing that, huh," she nods towards the snow-colored runway on his head.

"The more they remember you, the more they tip you," he says with a wink. His locker door creaks open.

"Um, hey," Bis gives a short laugh, shoving the door closed harder than necessary. "A bunch of us are heading to the Labyrinth tomorrow night after the Captain's gala. You in?"

Nova shakes her head. "I'm really..."

The locker door creaks open.

"Your locker okay?"

"Hmm? Sure, must not have closed it right." He pushes the door shut and keeps his hand there.

Nova shrugs it off. Bis was always up to something. She grabs a towel and a change of clothes from her locker, and heads to the showers.

Bis grins as she walks by, his eyes darting like those Earth rodents they keep in the petting zoo. Squirrels, she thinks to herself.

He's long gone when Nova returns to the locker room, pleasantly drowsy from her hot shower and dressed in comfortable clothes. A few other crew members are at their lockers, preparing for their shifts. Nova greets them but doesn't stop to chat. All she wants to do is to curl up in bed with a mug of hot tea and enjoy her biweekly vid-comm with Chuy. After that, she'll finally be able to activate the blackout setting in her cabin and get some sleep.

Nova drops a tea tab into a mug of water and within seconds the liquid is gently steaming. Cradling the mug in her hands, she settles cross-legged onto her bed. "Activate vid-com," she says and a screen on the wall blinks into life. "Initiate comm with Ch—" The door to her cabin suddenly slides open and Nova jumps to her feet, spilling her tea.

Cursing, she wipes her wet hands on her pajama shorts as she crosses the short expanse from her bed to the door. Leaning out, she sees nothing but empty corridor on both sides. Frowning, she taps the door control and watches it slide shut. Except for the *Ronnie's* Security Officers, who have ship-wide emergency clearance, Nova should be the only person able to access her room. She decides to wait until morning to submit a memo to Maintenance about the door glitch. With a sigh, she changes into a dry pair of shorts and climbs back into bed. "Initiate comm with Chuy."

"Hey, *bomboncita*," Chuy beams at her from the screen. He's leaning against their kitchen counter, a half-eaten empanada on the plate in front of him.

"*Hola*, handsome," Nova smiles at her boyfriend, then notices his food. "Oooh, I miss those." Chuy and his cousin run a luncheonette close to a major transport hub on their home planet. The empanadas are made with finely synthesized flour, hydroponic produce, cultured meat and a secret spice blend provided by Chuy's mom.

"Well, you can always jump ship and stay planet-side," he says, smiling. "I promise to make all the empanadas you can handle."

Nova laughs this off, but she knows Chuy isn't joking. Not really. They've been together for four years and for half that time she's been leaving to work long stretches on the starliner. She wishes she could say something to reassure him. Instead she asks, "How's the fam?"

Chuy rallies, "Good, we're all looking forward to your layover next week…" Something off to her right captures his attention. "Uh, Nova?"

She glances over her shoulder and sees nothing but pillows against the wall. One of which appears to be twitching. Nova sits back on her heels and grabs a hairbrush from the nightstand.

"Should you call Pest Management?" Chuy leans towards his screen as if trying to get a better look.

Gingerly, she pokes the now wriggling pillow with the hairbrush handle. A muffled yowl escapes the pillowcase, followed by a furry head shaped like an inverted triangle. Nova doesn't know which is more startling, the creature's luminous amber eyes or the oversized ears perched atop its head.

"¡Dios!" Chuy exclaims, his voice is mostly wonder, with a hint of disgust. "Is that a bat?"

Nova peers down at the little creature and shakes her head. "There's no wings."

"A wingless bat?"

Nova hesitates as she looks at the long slender tail curled around soft round front paws. "I think it's some sort of…cat."

"What kind of cat has ears like that?" Chuy's finger taps on the screen for emphasis.

"This one, apparently," Nova says. She reaches out her hand. The creature tilts its head up and walks forward, curving its back under her palm.

"She's so soft," Nova breathes as the warm fur glides beneath her fingers. The cat looks up smugly before circling around for another rub.

"Is she a petting zoo escapee?"

"No clue," Nova's finger snags on a small length of binding twine around the long neck, almost hidden beneath the white wavy fur. "But the zoo animals aren't collared and this twine is definitely from the *Ronnie*'s packing area." Nova looks up at Chuy's face, which by now, is so close that all she can see onscreen are the bushy twin arches of his eyebrows. "I think someone smuggled a pet on board."

"Oh, that's a big no-no. You gonna turn her over?" Chuy pulls back, and takes a bite of his empanada. Nova hears the crisp crunch of the fried batter and, for a moment, she imagines herself back home in their kitchen.

"First, I'm going to get this thing off her neck," Nova pulls open her nightstand drawer and grabs her nail clippers. The cat bounds into her lap and settles down, not even flinching as Nova snips off the twine.

"Second," Nova stifles a yawn. "I'm going to say *buenas noches* to you and get some sleep. I'll bring her to the Security Office in the morning."

***

Purr. Clink. Clink. Purr.

"Lights!" Nova yelps. 1,600 lumens of medium grade light slam into her eyes. She groans. In between blinks, she can see clothes scattered and bunched on the floor. Her room is tiny and it's clear that no one else is there. But, she does hear purring. She also notices that the small bowls of water and freeze-dried tilapia she'd set by the door are empty.

"Cat?" Nova calls out. The purring stops. A trail of clothing spills from the open closet door. Nova stumbles out of bed, rubbing her eyes, and bends down to pick up what used to be one of her freshly laundered starliner uniforms. There's a scattering of white cat hair on the black fabric.

"Cat?" she peers into the closet. A pair of amber eyes hover next to the floor safe.

Nova gets on her hands and knees and reaches in, ready to pull back her hand at the first sign of claws, but the white head raises in anticipation of a rub. Nova strokes the soft fur between the giant ears. "Boy, you're trouble, aren't you? Give me one good reason why I shouldn't march you down to Security right now."

The cat purrs, the sound rising and falling in sequence. There is a soft clink as the safe lock disengages, and the little metal door swings open.

Nova stares down at the cat. The cat blinks back.

The Observation Deck is on the top floor of the starliner, a whole cross section of the capsule-shaped ship with a glass ceiling viewable to the stars. Footpaths wind around several small gardens, cushioned loungers and couches positioned here and there. In the center of the all the flower gardens, herb gardens, and rock gardens, is the starliner's pride and joy; a labyrinth made of real *Ilex aquifolium*.

Esheserat scans her bracelet at the entrance and waits.

"Ah, welcome . . . Esheserat, the Reluctant Queen of Bronchitis." The words end in a gurgle as the Queen glares at the little man through yellow narrowed eyes. She knows a lazy maître'd when she sees one, like this fool feeding guests' names through the default medium grade e-translator. If he had taken the time and care to enter the syntax into a proper pronunciation calculator, a more accurate version of her title might have been, "Esheserat, Defiant Queen of the Fire-branching Wind Tunnels," a reference to the lava tubes that her home planet mined for rare fiber crystals.

Esheserat runs a nail along the soft ash-grey skin of her cheek. She hates these events, these new luxury starliner cruises, but Bis was right. This place is the best way a person of her status can blend in and do some less than noble business. On this eve of the Captain's dinner, with many well-dressed dignitaries milling about, perhaps a less than accurate name would be acceptable.

The little maître'd is lucky. Esheserat, the Reluctant Queen of Bronchitis, is in a good mood. A special delivery is coming very soon.

She steps past the little maître'd without a word, smelling the rank exhale of carbon dioxide as the little man lets out a long shaky breath.

***

The Reluctant Queen of Bronchitis makes her way along the paths, nodding at dignitaries in their finest silks and high-ranking officers in their impeccable dress whites, balancing champagne flutes and hors d'oeuvres in their hands. She pauses to touch the glossy leaves on one of the outer walls of the labyrinth, testing their pointed edges to see if they'll prick her skin.

"They're almost too shiny to be real, aren't they?" A rumbling voice inquires from behind her.

Esheserat takes a breath to soothe the irritation that arises whenever she's forced to make small talk. Her lips spread into her practiced and polished "meet'n'greet" smile as she turns around.

Captain Perry stands behind her, his grey hair slicked back, white uniform pressed and spotless. His hands are folded behind his back, making his chest puff and the medals on his chest stand out. She manages to keep the smile fixed on her face.

"Captain," she says. "What a delightful setting for your dinner. I was just admiring this beautiful labyrinth. We don't have much greenery on my planet, I'm afraid. Not many plants can survive the heat of our ground."

"I regret that I haven't had the pleasure of visiting your planet," the Captain says. "Not much vacation time running this ship."

"Really." She knows Perry's lying, about both being on her planet and the vacation time. "You must visit one day. It's quite different from this Earth experience. Beautiful, in its own way, glowing lava rivers and moss-covered plains," her voice tapers off.

"Have you seen the *Veronica Speedwell?*" He points to bunches of purple and pink flowers that line the walkways. "The ship's namesake."

"They're lovely," Esheserat says, ensuring there's just enough expression in her voice to sound impressed.

"If you'll excuse me your Majesty, I must make a few more rounds. Please enjoy your stroll through the garden," the Captain bows.

She watches as Perry walks away. He doesn't recognize her, she was only a girl back then, but she remembers him, remembers what he did. The dozens of miners he left behind in the tunnels, their lives worth less to him than the loads of crystal fibers taking their places in the transporter. The Queen curls her fingers into a fist, nails digging into her palm.

***

Esheserat strides down the corridor to her suite, relieved that the evening of exchanging inane pleasantries and ingesting bland Earth food is finally over. She hears a whirring of bike tires from behind and turns to see Bis. He pulls up beside her and dismounts, the bike's kickstand activating. She watches as the crewman with the ridiculous hair retrieves a package from the bicycle's carrier rack.

"The Ujimi pine oils you requested, your Majesty." Bowing slightly, Bis offers her the box.

Esheserat opens it and sifts through tissue until she sees the data device imprinted with the *Terran Transporters & Loaders* emblem. A flush of anger heats her face as old memories rise, but her voice is steady when she speaks.

"What excellent service," she says, "I'll see to it that a generous gratuity is credited to your account."

"Much appreciated, your Majesty." Bis bows again before hopping onto his bike and speeding down the hallway.

"Welcome to Sub-level 3, Security." the lift's cheery androgynous voice announces as the doors slide open with a hiss. Nova's last visit to the Security Office was years ago when she was hired to have her crew armbands coded and activated. It hasn't changed since then. The office is an homage to the American Police Station, circa 1980, with an open floor concept bullpen, worn beige linoleum, fluorescent tube lights flickering from the ceiling, and clunky metal desks topped with square terminal computers. Behind the bullpen is a row of offices, dusty blinds gaping in the windows.

It's early enough that even the bullpen desks are empty. Nova spies the small round shape of her friend Agril manning the front desk. Even though his Galivinian physiology allows him to go for days without sleeping, he looks wiped.

"Morning Agril, rough night?"

"Morning Nov," Agril shakes his bald head. "If anyone ever asks you to sub in as a maître d for an elaborate party, no matter how much extra they credit to your account just say—

Holy Hades, what is that thing?"

Nova smiles as she looks down at the white fur bundle in her arms. "A cat, I think. I wanted to see if anyone's reported her missing." The cat gently bumps her head against Nova's chin.

Agril lowers his voice, "Maybe bring her back later. The Captain's quarters were broken into last night. Something was stolen, but he won't say what, security footage was wiped and there's a lot of pressure for the Chief to find . . ."

"Giving away secrets of our investigation, ensign?" A voice booms from one of the offices. At seven feet tall, the Chief Security Officer's long legs take seconds to cross the bullpen and stand towering over the diminutive rotund ensign.

"Conveyance Crewman Dufau." The Chief's gruff tone makes Nova's spine stiffen. "As the ensign says, there was a break-in last night. The only evidence found at the scene was the hair of a very rare species." His eyes narrow at the pair of furred ears huddled in Nova's arms. "*Felis catus.*"

Nova swallows hard, wishing she had just given the cat more freeze-dried tilapia and gone back to bed.

"Please," The Chief motions with a hand, "Step into my office. We need to talk a few stories."

Nova cuddles the cat closer. Ignoring Agril's worried stare, she follows the Chief past the islands of empty desks into his office.

The door closes behind them.

Nova emerges from the Chief's office hours later, an aggrieved expression on her face. She passes Agril at the desk without seeing him. He scurries after her into the hallway.

"Nov? Are you well? Where's your cat? What did the Chief say?"

She waits until they're in the privacy of the lift to speak. "They're putting me off the ship at tonight's maintenance stop," she says, jabbing angrily at the lift buttons. "I've been relieved of duty upon suspicion of collusion."

Agril's mouth drops open in shock, "That's not right! You wouldn't do such a thing!"

"The Chief said I should consider it fortunate that nothing of the Captain's turned up when they searched my cabin." Nova shakes her head in disbelief. "But then, there's the cat."

"They can't spring to that conclusion because you happened to find the cat!"

"Well, they did." Nova says. "And it was actually the cat who found me. Listen, can you do me a favour?"

"Of course, yes."

"Please make sure she's taken care of. I can't stand the thought of her left in a storage area until they figure out what to do with her."

Agril nods vigorously, "Yes, I will do that. I will make sure she's taken care of."

"Thanks, Agril." The lift reaches her floor and Nova gives the small man a quick hug before exiting.

Nova waits by the loading area as the *Ronnie* pulls into Maintenance Bay 62. Agril is at her side, a security measure for the Chief, but Nova is glad for the friendly company in her final moments aboard the ship she's called home for years.

"Hey Nov," a voice says from behind them. They turn to see Bis step out of the shadows.

Agril looks between Bis and Nova, and raises an eyebrow. Nova nods.

"I'm going to, um, search your trunk one more time," Agril says. He waddles over to the jumbled pile of luggage and supplies waiting to be offloaded.

Bis watches the rotund little body walk a few steps away before turning back to face Nova. He shifts back and forth on his feet, uneasy. The light catches the white strip in his hair. It looks a little droopy today.

"That was your cat, wasn't it?" Nova says, breaking the silence.

Bis nods. "Thought I lost her last night. The Captain came back early and I had to half drag her back through the air vent. String got caught on a metal edge and she got loose."

"How does she...?"

Bis shrugs. "Best I can figure out? That cat in particular seems to be able to modulate the frequency of her purr and disrupt the locking mechanisms. Maybe she can hear something special with those ears."

"I hope it was worth it," Nova says, picking at her plain khaki jumpsuit. "Whatever it was you stole."

"Captain Perry's old ship logs, from back when he was a transport pilot. The proof needed to overcome his interplanetary immunity and finally have him arrested for some very shady dealings. It was for a good cause, Nov, honest."

Out of the corner of her eye, Nova sees Agril stiffen and stare at the luggage pile with wide eyes. A curved white tail is weaving and bobbing between corners of bags and edges of boxes. It stops by her trunk, and a few seconds later, the lid pops open. A white furry body with huge ears hops in.

Agril shoots her a grin as he closes the lid and re-secures the luggage lock with a flick of his wrist.

"It doesn't matter now," Nova shrugs, looking back at Bis, eyes brightening. "I think things might be better out there anyways."

And of course, she thinks with a smile, Chuy will be happy to have her back. He promised a hot platter of empanadas would be ready for dinner.

Ganymede Days

Victoria Feistner

Victoria Feistner is a writer, graphic designer, and artisan in equal parts, although some of those parts are more equal than others. A speculative fiction writer for over twenty years, she finished her first novel at age 18, and has been published in Syntax & Salt, Harbinger Press, The Future Fire, and GigaNotoSaurus, among other magazines and anthologies. Victoria lives in Toronto with her partner and two cats; examples of her work can be found at victoriafeistner.com.

The paint was peeling off the curved metal walls while the queue for meds snaked through the corridor, moving like a glacier, almost imperceptible to the eye. My gaze couldn't help being drawn to the flakes of off-orange, lifting away from the gun-gray composite underneath. First you ignore blistering paint during an inspection, then a hairline crack; eventually we're all pulled towards God and holding our breath 'til we burst as we do so.

The line shuffles forward.

New bodies ahead of me. Hotsteppers, in politer circles. Fleeing Earth's stagnation and hungry for purpose. Not yet used to Ganymede's low gravity so each footfall is ginger, like the metal tiles'll bite 'em or burn 'em. You can recog a hotstepper even when they're standing still: so *earnest*. Double-check their forms, wait patiently, then look surprised when they are turned away.

The kids are the worst: there's two. Still having fun; it's all so new. One waves to God or maybe she sees a ship.

My hands shake. I take a deep breath and stare at the broken paint.

Two mamas from 'stepping, that's me. Line-readers and plant movers, mostly. My parents' parents must have looked like this family, wide-eyed, bundled against the low temp, dizzy from the slightly low O2, afraid but hopeful all the same.

I hook a live fingernail under one of the flakes of paint and give it a twist, pulling it away.

The line shuffles forward.

An automaton rolls along-side, urging people to be more orderly and closer to the wall; in the slowness and boredom we've spread like mech grease into all available volume. Humanity in diorama.

The opposite wall is a bank of windows. Jupiter rises over Ganymede's small horizon, the brown-banded bulk filling our view, though God's eye not yet watching us. The hotsteppers ignore the automaton to lean towards the windows, entranced by the swirling clouds. Us Ganis, we stay near the wall, eyes darting to the nearest handhold each time we assume a new location.

Those of us that survived the riots, I mean.

Someone throws a meal can at the automaton. It doesn't slow or stop but part of its carapace rotates, scanning. A person might have narrowed eyes as they pick up the debris; it calmly extends a cleaning tube to disappear the can, its neutral voice requesting consideration.

Hunching my shoulders deeper into my coat gently pulls my dead hand inside the sleeve. I just want to fill my prescription and go back to my cube and my bed.

Ahead of me raised voices break the line as everyone else stops talking to stare. The two men shove each other, and the automaton reappears, blinking red, urging cessation.

This is all I goddamn need.

The deckherder's objecting to his prescription being denied. Either he hasn't paid the bribe or his gang's blacklisted but here we are. He's old enough to know how the moon spins but he's going to make it someone else's fault today: maybe the automata, maybe that newcomer family.

Maybe me, the half-and-halfer, dead fingertips still visible out of their coat sleeves, dead heart as close to hammering as its program ever lets it.

Just wanted to get my painkillers.

Two more automata, summoned like bad luck on a good day, roll up. But the deckherder's buddies are here too. Lifers pull back; hotsteppers crane.

I grasp the sleeve of the father, he's the closest to me, and shake him out of his snake-necking. "Go home," I urge. "Get your kids out of here. Come back tomorrow."

He looks me up and down, confused—I'm a head shorter, and a dozen kilos less massive—then realizes why my grip is so cold, too tight, and unyielding.

"You're one of them!" he says. And the asshole is beaming like a spotlamp, straight Earth teeth bright against his dark cheeks. "You're a motley!"

Heads turning. Watching me.

To lifers I'm an embarrassment, a symbol of how backward Ganymede still is. To new arrivals I'm personification of the '33 riots. To gangs like the one those deckherders cut themselves for, I'm an example of how the robot-loving government doesn't do enough to protect *real* people.

I break my grip and wipe my face with my live hand. "Go home, man, get your kids out of here."

But his eyes narrow. He turns to the automata while stepping away from me, shielding his kids from me, pointing. "She just threatened me!"

Shit.

Three automata, four deckherders bloated on steroids and stupidity, and one scrawny half-dead enby with a single painkiller left at home.

Both hands up. Heart thumping; so glad it decided to join the party.

The automaton, the one closest to me and the idiot tree-climber, whirrs its way over. It asks what happened and then one of the deckherder's chunkhead buddies throws a full meal.

At me.

The can misses by a meter to bounce off a pipe over my head.

The pipe is old; this quarter hasn't been inspected recently; the can hits with enough force to crack the aged and fragile plastic sealant. The noise of escaping gas prompts screams and shoves: a clever distraction, born of hisses signalling the worst kind of danger for generations.

And then one of the other deckherders pulls a taser. The automaton manages a squawk of errored-out surprise before it shuts down, sagging on its casing.

The other automata are on the deckherders in an artificial instant—tasers are illegal—but two of the bleeders manage to heave up the bulk of the fallen bot, arms straining from steroids meant to prevent muscle loss in the low G and abused in the name of chest-thumping masculinity.

Gravity is low but mass is constant.

On Earth, I've heard, an automaton wouldn't be liftable by four men, let alone two. But lift it they do, and he and his tattooed buddy hurl it like the primates they are.

All I can see is the smaller kid's face. He was fascinated by Jupiter rising. It was all so new. Delightful.

My dead hand reaches out to grab the kid by the front of his coat. My good hand grabs at his sister. I can lift things too, steroids or no steroids; I throw them to the closest handhold and hope they have the sense to grip.

The crack in the broken window spreads, jagged finger by jagged finger, epochally slow and yet as fast as the winds I'll fall up into.

The window breaks and the screams drown in the rush of air.

***

I open my eyes. Everything is raw and screaming but far away; it's a different person who hurts. I inhale: bad idea. Necessary but bad. My world is wrong somehow, flatter. I reach with dead fingers to my face and touch gauze instead of cheekbone or eyelid.

So.

The white-robed doctor comes in, their assistant automaton in gleaming silver. Seen that kindly look on doctor's faces before; the price of that expression was an arm, heart, and lung.

"How many lost?" I croak, my voice transmitted from somewhere outside the Oort, distorted and bundled in pharmaceutical swaddling.

"None," the automaton replied, sounding female to me. Or maybe it just sounded kind. "By blocking the breach with your body you saved the others."

I don't remember doing that. I do remember my ears popping and both sets of fingers clutching shards of glass.

"Unfortunately," the doctor continued, head tilted, hands crossed over the chart in their hands, "There were some complications from the decompression…"

I turn my head away from them. No windows here; good. I wouldn't want God to look down on me like this. To my right is a small locker. There's a bottle of pills with my name and number on it, my prescription filled after all.

I close my live eye. I can feel the phantom sliver of paint under my fingernail. Even in my drug-sogged haze the sensation is vivid and encompassing.

These are the little moments that I'll remember, as Ganymede takes me apart piece by bloody piece.

On the Cusp of Darkness

C.L. Holland

C.L. Holland is a British writer of science fiction and fantasy, and has been published in magazines and anthologies such as Daily Science Fiction, Cats in Space, and Nature Futures. She has a BA in English with Creative Writing, and MA in English. When not working or writing she can be found making jewellery, or reading about history and folklore.

It was the cusp of dawn when I reached the village, that strange half-light before the sun reaches the horizon. Early enough to show my allegiance, late enough not to offend the villagers' sensibilities. They were rarely welcoming to those who knocked on their doors in the dark hours.

Lights burned above every door, lanterns and candles proclaiming the relative wealth of the occupants, warning me away. All except for one house, where the lantern was dark and the door open in invitation.

There, then.

A dim light came from inside, and I slipped into a circle of candlelight with a short, grey-haired woman at its centre. She would be mother or grandmother, or the nearest female relative, which meant it was a girl I'd come to claim if I could. I wasn't sure whether to be pleased or pity the poor creature. My order was woefully short of female members, but in my experience girls were harder to talk around than boys.

The woman greeted me with a nod and shielded the candle with her hand. The action surprised and pleased me, even though I wasn't so bound to Darkness that the meagre light would hurt.

"She's in there," the woman started, nodding towards a narrow door.

The front door slammed wide open behind me, and a tall man burst through. His close-cropped blond hair glistened with sweat in the light of the lantern he held high. I resisted the urge to shield my eyes as he waved it at my face.

"She's staying there."

I raised my eyebrows. "Unless you're the girl's mother, you have no say in this."

"I'm her father, and I won't have her dragged out of here by a whore of Darkness."

Inwardly, I sighed. The old argument, trotted out by fathers, uncles, and brothers who feared what Darkness had to offer. "I'll remember your wishes if Darkness ever sends me for your son," I promised, and left him to wonder how I knew he had one. "But my business here is with the girl and her closest female relative."

"She's not closest," he said triumphantly. "She's my wife's mother."

I turned an enquiring look to the grandmother.

"Don't you worry girl, it's been done proper," she said. "I told Mirley, you do right by that girl or you'll regret you didn't. She couldn't do it herself, so she gave up rights to Sirsa before I summoned you. She's yours to take, if you'll have her."

"It's up to her to choose," I reminded.

"The priests are already on their way," the father blurted. "They'll be here with the sun."

I turned to face him, my anger with his pig-headedness rising.

Too many times well-meaning parents thought to take the choice from their children's hands, casting them into the care of the priesthood before anyone could explain to them what being marked by Darkness actually meant. I let it fill me, knew that my eyes went black and speckled with stars like the night sky. The girls' father quailed as the candle went out and his lantern dimmed to a pinprick.

"Well then," I said cheerfully. "I'd best get started."

Beyond the narrow door, the air was dry and herb-scented. Steps led away beneath my feet and I stifled a laugh. They'd locked a child of darkness in a cellar?

As I made my way down, the door slammed closed behind me. There were raised voices, Sirsa's father and grandmother arguing. Obviously he'd chosen to lock an adept of the Dark in the cellar too, no doubt hoping the priest would take care of me when they came for his daughter. He wouldn't be so lucky: my choice had already been made.

The cellar had a packed dirt floor and was lined with shelves on which sat jars of pickles and preserves. Bundles of herbs hung from the ceiling, and sacks were piled in the corner like sleeping puppies. For a moment I wondered where Sirsa was. Then I saw her, a patch of dark against darkness underneath the table in the corner. There was a makeshift mattress of sacks beneath her, rumpled and spilling straw.

"Go away!" Her voice was shrill with fear.

I stopped and reached for the low stool, sat down near enough that she would hear me. She turned towards the noise, her senses not yet developed enough to see me clearly. I could see her, nine or ten years old with brown hair that curled behind her ears.

"Do you know why I'm here?" I asked softly.

"You've come to take me away. You'll tear me into strips and feed me to the Darkness, that's what Myram said!"

"And how would Myram know?" I asked softly. "Is he an adept of the Dark?"

"No!" She flinched. "Papa says only sick people choose the Dark. There's something wrong with them and—" She broke off, probably remembering who she was talking to.

"Your time is short, you know that," I told her. "Your father has already summoned the priests. When the sun rises you'll either have come with me or with them. Which happens is your choice, but it's the only choice you have." It wasn't, running and suicide had also been chosen in the past, but I didn't want to put that idea into her head. "Do you know what will happen when the priests come?"

"They'll put me in an asylum. Papa said they could make me better but Gramma said he was lying. She said they'd hurt me."

"They might," I agreed. "It depends on what sort of priests they are. Some would see you as a victim of the Dark, cursed through no fault of your own. They would keep you gently. Others would see you as a willing accomplice to your own corruption and try to purify you. It some cases, that can hurt."

My fingers sought the smooth, tight flesh on my forearms. I knew firsthand what "purification" could mean. Too much sunlight would burn anyone, but at noon when there were no shadows to hide in, then it could do more than burn us. Worried I'd frightened her, I added, "The monks in the nearest monastery are the gentle sort."

Sirsa had shifted to look at me. She was chewing a fingernail. I pretended I couldn't see her.

"You don't sound mad," she allowed. "Why did you choose the Dark?"

"Because-" I broke off. It was a long time ago, when I was thirteen and wilful. "My parents told me not to," I said finally. "They told me I was mad, too. They wanted me to go with the priests and be cured and come home to marry."

"But you didn't."

"No. I wanted more than that. The Dark offered me a way to have it."

She retreated a little, and I wondered if I was losing her. Most girls chose the priests over the Dark from fear of letting their family down. Fear that they really were mad. Signs of the Dark in them were an aberration and showed weakness of character. For boys it was different somehow, less of a taint. I wished I could make her understand. Being marked by the Dark wasn't good or bad, any more than the sun set was good or bad; it just *was*.

I slipped from the stool onto the floor to be on her level. She was huddled against the wall, knees up to her chin. There was a rag-doll on the spilled straw beside her.

What kind of parents locked their child in a cellar but let her keep a doll for company?

"Sirsa," I said, "why did your parents lock you in here?"

"They didn't," she said.

"Then who made that bed for you?"

"I did. I stuffed the sacks myself, to make a bed." There was a note of childish pride in her voice. My heart constricted. She'd already made her choice but didn't know it.

"Why?"

"Because sometimes, if I can't sleep or if I'm scared, I come down here." Her hand found the ragdoll and clutched it tight.

"Does it help?"

She nodded. "I can get to sleep then."

"Doesn't the lantern keep you awake."

"I don't bring a lantern," she said scornfully. I saw her expression change as she realised. "Oh."

In the distance there was the tolling of a handbell. The priests had come. Sirsa looked up at me, her eyes wide.

I met her gaze and saw her surprise as she realised I could see her. "There's no more time," I said. "I wish I could show you somehow, it's not as terrible as you think."

She shook herself. "What will happen if I go with you?"

"We'll help you find out what gifts the Dark gave you, teach you how to control and make the best of them."

"But everyone will be afraid of me. I'll never see my family again. I don't care about Myram, but I'll miss Mam and Gramma."

"You'll see them if they're not afraid." It wasn't much of a con-solation, since most people were afraid, but I'd wager than her grandmother would see her in a heartbeat. "If they are, well, that's not likely to change whatever you choose. Even if you come back 'cured,' they'll still fear you."

She sighed. "It's not fair."

"I know."

She took my hand. "You promise no one will hurt me?"

"No one will lay a hand on you if you do not wish for it. I swear by the Dark."

She gave a small smile and edged out from underneath the table to take my hand. Her fingers were cold but her grip firm. We both flinched as the door swung open in a glory of light.

The priests made way for us, grudgingly, although they made sure their light shone fully on me as we passed. Just because they were the gentle sort of priest didn't mean they felt any softness towards those who chose to be an adept of the Dark over a life of confinement. I kept Sirsa safely in my shadow.

Her grandmother was waiting outside, she nodded to me and hugged Sirsa tightly. Her father was waiting too, his lips pinched into a thin line. When Sirsa hugged him I thought he'd push her away, but instead he drew her close and I heard him murmur, "Please don't go, flower."

"I have to, Papa," she whispered back. "I have to find out what I can do."

The sun had just barely cleared the horizon. Sirsa frowned towards it as she turned back to me. "But where will we go? It's nearly daytime."

"Most of us can go out in the day."

"Oh. I didn't know that."

There was a pause as we began to walk. Then, "Why can't the rest go out in the day?"

That was a lesson for later but I began to tell her what I could, as we walked away from the ragdoll and the straw-stuffed mattress where she'd chosen her future.

First appeared in *Cucurbital* 2, November 2012

Luminous

Kel Purcill

Kel Purcill is an Australian PhD student, following her Honours focus on addressing the cultural erasure of women through science-fiction. Kel has published fiction, creative non-fiction, poetry and academic essays in literary journals, anthologies and magazines internationally. She's on Twitter @ SelwynsSanity

Like many modern fairy tales, Shaz's happily-ever-after wasn't. After a crunchy, bloody uncoupling, she had no interest in potential princes or frogs, focussed only on how to banish the ghost of her marriage which lingered like a confused spell. She cast her long forgotten magics, hesitant and unfamiliar, learning again of luxuriating in the depth of her unshared mattress, the forgotten delight of shopping for one, and being entirely content in shaving what and when she wanted.

Divorce suited her. She painted her toenails blue, the letter box fuchsia, caught up with friends he'd hated, enjoyed work lunches and tried to grow mint. A friend sent her a massage voucher which read 'Congrats on surviving Small Dick-Major Arsehole syndrome'—she had it framed and hung beside her bathroom mirror. She was happy, divorced, and waking each night, delighted, to bake.

Each night's whim created a different dish. Custard pie on a Tuesday when she'd seen a fire truck full wail, lemon crepes after a purple-heavy sunset, chilli chocolate shortbread celebrating the wondrous word 'amok'. Leaves budded and unfurled outside as the pages in her recipe book grew loose and lovely, butter and summer soon sitting on her benchtop, gingerbread sprawling in brown sugar syrup on odd midnights when she woke laughing, pavlova in jewelled glory after rain.

Shaz was swaying to thick jazz one summer night, a vanilla pod snuggling in coconut cream on the counter, when the moon walked down from the sky and knocked quietly on her veranda door.

"I've bought you some sugar—Tahitian brown." She shone, earnest and dark haired.

"How lovely," Shaz beamed. "Uh, can I get you some water?"

They chatted while she made vanilla bean cheesecake, the moon's laughter rolling into the kitchen cabinets and bewitching the cat. The moon left with a luminous slice tucked sweetly into napkin origami, while the star she nestled in Shaz's fruit bowl cast dreams on the blue ceiling as the dawn yawned awake.

The moon, invited, came again the next week, this time calling a low hello through the thrown wide windows, open to the crickets' raspy gossip and cool breezes. They compared days—Serbia needed rain, white Queensland beach sand was still between Shaz's toes—and discussed books as the moon stood beside her at the sink, drying mixing bowls while tiny tides shifted the bubbles between them. They sat outside eating dimpled pikelets, cherry jam and cream with their fingers while the sky spilled nebulas above their heads, unnoticed.

"May I see you again, in four days?" the moon asked, turning at the front fence, watching as Shaz pushed, released, pushed, released the gate latch.

"Please, yes," she nodded, eyes creasing into shadows, "I'd like that."

Anticipation fizzed and swirled across the coastlines, pooling in the pauses of their days, the moon's hauling in a monsoon's deluge, hers coordinating staff and volunteers for the next blood donation drive. The days dragged, sped, yanked by gravity and nerves, until finally the gate latch clicked and sung at her arrival, within earshot of where Shaz was watering the mint with distraction and an enthusiastic hand.

They smiled, hellos tangling, then turned to the drowning mint.

She swore, crimping the hose. "Dammit, I'm killing it with kindness."

"Not a bad way to go, really."

It was early evening when she'd arrived, cloudy streamers and glitter still piled close to the horizon, the day's humidity finally uncurling from Shaz's neck. The moon shucked her shoes off towards the clothesline, then wrestled the unruly hose in Shaz's wake. Their conversation waltzed between the garden beds—the existence of aliens considered while they splashed their feet mostly clean, the spicy kick of the cardamom biscuits fuelling the best-action-movie-of-all-time debate, chilled glasses of milk somehow leading to a joke about clowns in high heels. Later, after midnight, stretching like a starfish in bed, Shaz couldn't remember the punchline but still fell asleep smiling.

The moon is wooing, went the whisper abroad, *somewhere in Australia.* Fishermen, long used to the moon's conversation while waiting for the catch, found themselves leaning, instead, towards the velvet waves, finally seeing the violet and blue life flickering far beneath. Astronomers fretted, discordant, scrawled the moon notes, stuck them to telephone poles, demanding an end date to the madness...only to send thank you kites weeks later, in gratitude for the unimagined clarity of distant nebulas. Star gazers—professional, amateur and newly intrigued—grew pale and energised by their night time endeavours, hearing starsongs in their sleep, not missing midday's bright traffic and hum in the slightest.

Independence suited Shaz. She drove up to a hinterland dairy on a day off, just to remind herself what a cow looked like. She hunted for second-hand bookstores, found delicious spices in tiny supermarkets, said no without explanation. Summer waned while she waxed more luminous, settling deeper into her own skin, fine-tuning her recipe for happiness. The ingredients changed regularly, but often included butter, purples, record numbers of community blood donations, crushed mint, the neighbourhood kids waving hi, a new bookcase...and starshine.

The moon continued her woo. Sailors at sea, blinking after molasses nights, enquired courteously after her lady as she climbed back into the sky, dusted with flour and—soon—kisses smudging the corners of her mouth.

They learnt each other's rhythms, moods and delights. The moon came bearing Armenian cherries one leaf-tossed evening and fed them to Shaz, purple staining her lips, inking their fingers, a distraction from the ache in Shaz's back, the weight of her hips, the temporary rhythm of flux and ebb. The next week, here, Shaz scorched marshmallows outside, blowing out the caramelised flame in the distant direction of the moon's now wiry shoulder, pale and curved towards a distant continent. There, she watched sugar cane burn, and tasted Shaz on her tongue.

When she returned, days later, Shaz fed her soup while straddling her lap. Shaz held the bowl, she cupped Shaz's backside, both marinating in the relief of them being in her kitchen again, at night, sugar and stars sparkling, together. They shared a slice of rum-spiked sweet potato bundt cake.

Shared the fork.

Shared a kiss.

Shared a pillow.

"No, not dawn," Shaz groused against her moon's neck, much later, tasting her skin again. 'Where is the lovely moon?'

The moon sucked the curve of Shaz's breast, slid her hand up the unshaved horizon of Shaz's thigh.

"She is way, way laid"—a grin, a hot lick against Shaz's belly—"and about to make breakfast."

She made Shaz shakshouka, made her laugh, made her a packed lunch while she showered, and then, when Shaz searched for underwear, ate at her mouth, her neck, until she dropped the towel. They were both late for work, then, luscious and sated.

The moon knows now where her secret freckles are, how books throw her into ecstatic motion, her stomping offense at ants in the kitchen. Shaz now knows the curls of her body, her devotion to indie rock, how weary she has sometimes been climbing into the heavens.

Happiness suits her. Suits them both, as entwined and synchronous as they are, slow dancing in the kitchen, enthusiastic with their careers, making messes and meaning and magic together, content within the staggered weaving of their weeks. Shaz is in cosy pyjamas painting her toenails jacaranda, the first fig and ginger pudding of the season steaming softly when the moon carefully delivers a scrawled baklava recipe from her adopted nonna. A Greek woman living in Delphi, draped in midnight folds and wrinkles, who has demanded wildly across the page 'grow fat with love, be happy, use butter, everyday'.

They do. Her neighbours cheerfully buy thicker curtains for the rooms facing her fence or shift their beds so the lovelight doesn't shine so directly in their faces, all carefully arranging pillows and curtain folds so the tides of sugar, carbs and moondust are free to wash in, to ebb around their midnights, to perfume their dreams.

The Anatomy of Spines

Nikki Kroushl

Nikki Kroushl (sometimes writing as Nicole Crucial) is a graduate of UNC Wilmington's BFA program in creative writing. Much like a houseplant, she loves sunlight, the indoors, astrology poems, and when the cat sits next to her on the window sill. Read her work at nicolecrucial.com.

Lorelei was so close I could barely breathe: a leftover habit from days when we shared one sleeping bag. She had her sharp nose buried in my neck. Her fingernails pressed a thin staircase of white lines into my hip, clutching at me as if she would like to climb inside me. She'd have made quite the little home in the zipper of my spine; she would have been comfortable among the teeth.

I turned over, interrupting her protest with a kiss.

"Good morning," I said.

"Happy birthday," she answered, "and I'm sorry for your loss."

"No loss. Not yet."

"Rosco."

"I told you I won't do it."

***

Our teacher, Elias, first tried to explain it to me when I was small. The classroom: a circle of stones worn flat by centuries of bottoms, old snow churned to green-gray slush, other children ushered into the creek and encouraged to savage its newly cracking ice. *Rosco, stay behind, I need to speak with you. No, you're not in trouble.*

I cupped my palms over my knees. I stared after my friends, who tumbled over one another and tore at each other's coats in the haste to smash the ice and smother the silver fish underneath. A weight, a crash, a reckless abandon, a failure to know anything but all of the above.

Elias explained about lines, simplicity, the order of things, blood, burials, necessity, mothers. *Usually it's fathers,* he said, *but your case is special.*

I didn't look at him. Instead I watched Lorelei pull a fish out of the stream. She'd skewered it on three of her claws; red spots glistened in a row like buttons. She could have undone them one by one to reveal muscle, bone, a buried sachet of eggs. She retracted her claws, dropped the fish into her palm. She grinned as our classmates gathered around her, poking the feverish fish and the blood that ran over her hands.

She met my eyes. She smiled wider. It was the first time I saw her smile.

Elias tilted his head, scratching forlorn at the gray whiskers of his jaw. He said, *Are you paying attention?*

I wasn't.

***

"Rosco," Lorelei said. "You have to."

"I'm a special case." I pulled on my jeans.

"*We're* a special case," she answered. She reached out, linked her fingers through mine, pulled me back to face her.

She pressed my hand to her chest, over the tiny carved minnow that hung against her collarbones. Little fish, smaller than a coin, strung on a piece of leather.

"Yes," I said. "But."

"You're always swimming upstream."

***

To me, as a seven-year-old, it seemed she arrived out of nowhere. The necklace she had when she came wasn't the minnow—I made that for her, later, after the first smile. The one she came with was a little sparrow, half in flight.

Lorelei was always half in flight, too. Her claws emerged at every sudden half-sound. Her teeth sharpened at a millisecond's notice, grew too large for her to close her lips. Her transformations were faster and meaner than they had a right to be. She always needed new clothes and old patience. Only one of those things could be bought in inland towns, under the duress of winters biting harder each year.

At a Pack dinner one evening, I decided it was my job to make her laugh. I molded my mashed potatoes into a pile and spooned them onto my face: a butter-drenched beard.

Lorelei sat across from me, ensconced near the center of the long table. On either side of her, adults called comments to friends across the tables. Lorelei sat with her head down, eyes locked on her food.

My mother was distracted, discussing something about borders. I had limited time so I hissed: "*Lorelei.*"

She looked up. Her blue eyes went wide. She stared at my potato-smeared chin, then down at my plate, then into my eyes.

Her face was frozen, frozen, frozen—and then cracked. The smallest tightening of her mouth, an upturning at the corners of her lips.

My mother groaned beside me.

"Rosco," she said, sighing. "Gods almighty. Why?"

I didn't answer, even as she dragged me away by the ear to scrub my cheeks raw.

***

I let Lorelei pull me back to bed.

"This is what she wants," she said.

"It's what she tells herself she wants."

"How is that any different?"

Outside: the aching, oblivious trills of small birds. A beautiful summer day. A beautiful day to die, if somebody could choose.

"What do you want?" I asked her.

She moved my hand from her chest to her cheek. Her skin under my palm looked so soft, but it was roughened by the endless days of buffeting wind.

"You," she said.

"That's what you tell yourself you want," I said.

"Fine," Lorelei admitted. "I want you. And I want to run this place by your side as consort. And I want our people to be happy and to prosper and to be strong. I want to protect this place."

I stayed quiet.

"I want you to be the best leader we've ever seen," she said, her voice dropping a few decibels. "And I want you to be happy."

I shook my head.

"You're right," Lorelei continued. Now she skimmed the pads of her fingers down my bicep, stroked the back of my hand. "Your mother doesn't want to die. But she wants all those things. She wants you to be Alpha."

"It's not what I want."

***

My mother sat cross-legged in a clearing on a summer day near my seventh birthday, the breeze lifting her cropped curls. A mother is always something like a fairytale. Ethereal. Impossible. Beautiful.

They brought Lorelei to her. Led the wild-haired, sharp-toothed child practically into her lap, until she stood with her toes six inches from my mother's knees.

"Hello," she said.

"Hello," Lorelei answered.

My mother refused to whisper around Lorelei as the other adults did. Did not take special care to eradicate words from her vocabulary like *slaughter, hiding, mother, blood*. She believed no word should get exceptional treatment.

"You will live with us now," my mother said. "I'm not sure if you'll like it, but it's what will be."

Lorelei continued to stare.

"Tragedy makes you iron," my mother said. "Do you understand?"

Lorelei didn't answer. But never, never did I see her bend.

***

I left the cabin and Lorelei in our bed. Outside the sun did nothing to warm my skin or my gut. I tracked across the curving bare path to my mother's cabin, five hundred feet away.

I knocked; she opened the door. I expected, at least, dark purple circles under her eyes, a beaten dull color to match the strands of gray in her hair. She stood as calm and impassive as ever, dressed for the day as if it were any other day.

"Good morning," she said. "Happy birthday."

"Hardly," I said.

***

I first kissed Lorelei when we were eleven years old. It made sense—survivor of one Pack, heir of another. We were inevitable. We didn't want to believe it was sensible: we wanted to believe it was desperate, doomed, forbidden. We were frustrated when my mother and the other adults caught us kissing and walked by, amused.

When we were eleven, the kissing was childish. By thirteen we'd moved on to the desperate, handsy, clawing stuff you could expect from any kids our age. We were sick of being two separate people: we wished we could fuse our bodies.

Our people aren't talkative. Lorelei especially—who idolized my mother—preferred to speak with actions. The pads of her fingers, ever-present on the insides of my wrists. The pressure of her chin resting on my shoulder. The quiet kisses in my hair, almost absentminded, which invariably sent awed chills rolling down my chest. She rarely spoke her feelings, but I almost never wondered how she felt.

"I love you," I told her when we were fourteen.

She smiled. "Of course."

I frowned.

"Do you love me?" I asked her. The only time I ever did.

She folded my palms into hers and lifted to her toes and kissed me, slow and deep and smoldering.

"I do," she answered. "I always will. You are the other half of my soul. I don't know who I am without you."

Soft warmth poured over my skin, making me want to shed layers even in the subzero temperatures.

"Why do you love me?" I asked her, just fishing at this point. I thought.

She rolled her eyes. Smirked.

"I love you for who you are."

***

My mother invited me to sit across from her at the huge slab of tree trunk that stood in the cabin—half coffee table, half center of command.

"I won't do it," I told her.

"You must."

"What kind of leader takes orders from his mother?"

"A good one."

I gripped the arms of the rocking chair, trying not to remember lullabies, my forehead under her chin, being small enough to fit completely in the crowding of her elbows. I didn't say, *I can't take orders from my mother if she's dead.*

"I don't want this."

"Why would you?" she replied. "And why should that change anything?"

"Surely the Pack doesn't want an Alpha who doesn't want this," I said.

"No," she said, "but they want you more than someone who does want it."

***

Lorelei never outgrew the idea that love is just constancy, that *always* is short for *always here*, that being mutually consumed in something heady and suffocating is the highest expression of *forever*. Love became an exercise in balancing the vacuum of her desire, her need, with my speeding heartbeat, which had less to do with arousal and more to do with panic.

***

"You'll meet me at the river," my mother said.

As she passed me, she let her fingers fall on the back of my neck. The lightest touch, the roughest fingers. I felt a thrum of warmth, a desire to lean in—but her nails were cold and knife-sharp on my spine.

Lorelei thumbed the minnow around her neck, worrying the tiny, clumsy scale details smooth.

"It's a new beginning," she said.

"That's not what it feels like."

"So dramatic."

"It would be the end of everything."

She paused. Her fingers dropped lower, tracing the fabric of her shirt between her breasts, where I knew the sparrow still hung hidden.

"The end of everything is much worse than you know," she said.

"Lorelei, I didn't mean that."

"You always do, whether you know it or not."

"I am no fool," I said. "I would never compare one death to hundreds. I would never compare the loss of a mother to the loss of a people."

"But," she said.

"But this is my personal nightmare."

"It's your birthright," she said.

"I never wanted this."

"I never wanted to be a lone survivor," she said. Breathing heavy but even. "I thought..."

"What?"

"If you were an orphan, too, you might understand."

My lungs were not my own: she was inside my ribcage, breathing with me, for me, instead of me.

"Why would you ever want me to understand what that feels like?"

"I'm selfish," she answered, easily. "And so are you."

***

Riverbank. In the water next to us, dozens of oblivious silver fish. A crowd, gathered.

"Ready?" she said.

"No."

My mother nodded. A hand sailed down in lieu of a flag. She closed the gap between us in half a second. By then she was half-transformed—her jaw elongated, body hunched and furred, teeth and claws at ready.

Her palms-paws collided with my chest, knocking me to the ground. An animal roar escaped her. The rancid heat of her wolf's breath blew in a dizzying fog around my face.

My body shook with tension. I let her knock me down, let her hiss. I dug my fingers into the leaf litter underneath me and willed the instinctive sharp points of claws to slide back underneath my cuticles.

She stopped. She didn't tear my throat out. I hadn't expected her to—still, some small part of me feared she was exactly as ironclad as she appeared to the world.

She made a growling, guttural noise that sounded vaguely like: *Fight back.*

"No," I whispered, so only she could hear.

"*Rosco!*" Lorelei screamed from the sidelines. I didn't take my eyes off my mother's yellow irises, but I could sense the heat-movement-struggle, the many hands pinning Lorelei's arms to her sides and barring her from the fray. "Rosco, *fight her!*"

"No," I whispered again, even more quietly.

My monster-mother rose, looking down on me now from a distance of two feet instead of two inches. She lifted one furred, heavy arm and slapped me.

My cheek opened underneath her nails and stung with the gush of hot blood and flecks of dirt. I howled, and I could feel my nails curving outward again, my jaw cracking, desperate to stretch into slavering maw.

When I still didn't react, she climbed off me. She fought her wolf features, packed them away into herself chunk by chunk, till she had returned to a petite woman with gray-streaked hair in stretched-out, dirtied clothing.

"Coward," she said, her voice carrying in echoes, drowning out the sound of the water, the ignorant minnows. "Weakling. You are not my son."

I closed my eyes against the betraying blue of the sky and let the open wound in my face weep.

***

Lorelei, stitching my face closed with clumsy, unpracticed

hands: always the fighter, never the healer. My mother's child, more than I ever was.

"It will scar," she said. "That's good. It will remind you."

"You're just like her."

"That's no insult."

"I know."

"Why didn't you fight?" Her fingers tender now, my hair sliding between them. She kept her other hand on her chest, pressing the carved minnow.

"I don't want to. And," I added before she could object, "I can't. I am no fighter. She would kill me."

"She's your mother."

"She doesn't believe in pulling punches."

"Believe me, as someone 'just like her.' She wouldn't kill you."

The dust motes danced in the late-afternoon light. The world inside our cabin was insulated. I didn't want to think about what awaited me among the Pack outside: there was no place for me anymore. My mother bore a son too early, and she was so young to have an adult heir already. If I had really killed her, they'd have hated me. But they must have hated me more for failing to kill her. For failing them: for failing the age-old rituals which had kept us hot-blooded in centuries of tundra winters.

"What do you see for us?" I said. I laid my hands on Lorelei's hips. "Someday. A family?"

"Yes," she said. A cautious glow hovered over those blue eyes. I never wanted to talk about the future.

"How many kids?"

"Well, the one is traditional," she said. "I wouldn't mind another, if it wouldn't complicate...things. Or we could make like your mother and take in a stray."

"You're always swimming upstream," I said. I thumbed the necklace at her throat.

She caught my hand. Moved it to her breast. She leaned in with a heated, breathless smile. Her cheekbones shined with the day's washes of adrenaline, terror, the warm pressure of love.

She kissed me, touching her lips to mine with an agonizing slowness. My hand, still on her hip, squeezed involuntarily. Lorelei swung her left leg over my legs and lowered herself into my lap, gentle-careful not to touch the stitches in my cheek.

We'd spent so many afternoons this way: bathed in the mellow light, kissing and fucking the afternoon away as if we had all the time in the world.

"The one, traditional child," I said. "She grows up to kill me."

Lorelei froze.

"A long way off," she said.

"Not long enough," I said.

"This is how things are. This is how we have done things."

"Centuries ago. When the Packs were always at war, when our people wanted leaders to prove they could be ruthless and sacrifice anything to win. Things aren't the same."

"Your mother believes differently."

It didn't matter that, on an intellectual level, above the ache in my chest, I knew that Lorelei didn't want me to kill my mother, that she just wanted what she thought was best for me. And us.

"I will not kill her," I told her. "Whatever it takes. If I have to leave, become a lone wolf, live with humans in the city—"

"Rosco," Lorelei said. "Don't talk like that."

I touched her face. I ran a thumb along her jaw. She frowned, recoiling at what must be unusual pressure there, a tension I couldn't shake even when I wanted to be gentle.

"I'm serious," I said. "I'm sorry, Lor, but I will never, never give you what you want. If...when, someday, my mother leaves this earth, it won't be because of me."

***

I woke at dawn. I lingered under the blankets, unmoored in the sense of being awake before I needed to be. I rolled over, letting the battery-powered heater go a while longer.

Then I felt it. My body locking at the joints. My breath gone, lungs sucking in on themselves. An emptiness tore open my chest—I couldn't move, couldn't breathe, couldn't think—

But I knew then, without knowing. *Mom.*

I shot out of bed like a vampire out of noon sunlight, like a silver bullet out of a sawed-off shotgun.

I sprinted across the worn ground in bare feet. I ripped my mother's door off its hinges and flung it, ignoring the splinters.

My mother lay on the ground, cheek in dirt, misleading delicate curls clotted with blood. Blood streaked down her back, soaked her nightclothes, gushed out of inch-thick, glistening gouges that showed the pale shattered bones beneath.

And there, beside her: Lorelei. Her chest heaved. She crouched over my mother, disheveled and feral. The minnow and the sparrow had both come loose, hanging in front of her black shirt.

Two of Lorelei's fingers were buried in a deep hole in my mother's neck. Her other hand lifted into the air as she turned to look at me. Her fingers stained red. I remembered the river, the fish. Her almost surgical deconstruction of its body, the glee with which she speared its flesh. The first time I'd seen her smile. She didn't smile now.

And I was still, again.

Without inhaling or breaking eye contact, Lorelei sank her claws an inch deeper. My mother still did not move.

I waited to feel it. The bubbling red heat. The razors bursting from my fingertips, the teeth crowding my jaw, the snap of bones reforming and springing toward her.

My fingers twitched. My shoulders convulsed, an uneven flinching that forced me to take a step back. The building pressure at the nape of my neck, then—nothing.

Lorelei rose. Aside from her hands, she was painfully clean: just a few flecks of blood across her cheeks and shirt, blending into the dark color. She straightened and took one slow step toward me, as if testing the water.

I was somewhere else—watching from some space outside my body—I couldn't move it, could only watch her, numb in the head, as she took two more steps. One more, until she was close, and I could smell the blood.

She smeared the blood across my bare chest with trembling hands. With the two fingers that had sliced through my mother's spine, she drew splattered lines across my cheek. She flicked her fingers out in a fanned shape, so that droplets danced across my stomach and shoulders. She pulled my hands from the clenched fists at my sides and undid my fingers, smearing them red in long strokes. I imagined her scrawling words with her fingertips, writing gods knew what.

The red was an unmistakable brand, bright and shining against my skin. Almost serene in her movements, Lorelei stepped away from me. She found the wash basin in the corner of the room and rinsed the thick viscous red from the creases in her palms. She baptized her hands.

Outside, the Pack's voices began to swell.

***

Lorelei is so close I can barely breathe. Her sharp nose buries in my neck. Her fingernails press a thin staircase of white lines into my hip, clutching at me as if her limbs were a finely wrought cage. She learned the anatomy of spines from these long-night embraces: she discovered just how to reach in and unzip.

Every night I dream about that morning: the icy arrest of knowing, the sprint across the path, the standing there, watching Lorelei sever the last thread that connected my mother to life. My mother would have been proud of her. Sometimes, in my dreams, the boiling red overwhelms me, my jaw snaps, my claws lurch forward, and I skewer an open-mouthed Lorelei under the ribs: the strings of her necklaces caught between my impaled fingers. On those nights, she chokes and gurgles and stills next to my mother.

A Life in Six Feathers

Kathryn Yelinek

Kathryn Yelinek is a librarian and writer. She grew up in Pennsylvania and, with the exception of a few short stays elsewhere, have lived there all her life. She earned a master's degree in library science and when not writing, spends her days working in a university library. Like many librarians, she has a tendency to be overly helpful.

I. Down feathers—the foundation layer, which underlies most other feathers

Abby let the dented screen door slap closed behind her. "Mom, I'm home!"

She plastered on her best grin to deflect any mom-scowls over the screen door. But the house was quiet. Only Einstein, her parakeet, warbled happily from her bedroom.

Abby frowned and dropped her schoolbag on the rental-beige carpet. In the kitchen, a note sat next to the half-finished sink of dishes. *Sorry, Abs, we'll have to go to the zoo another time. I got called in. Happy Birthday!*

The crumpled note bounced off the rim of the trashcan. Abby stomped on it and tossed it in. She stomped to her bedroom.

"Divorce sucks," she told Einstein, who chortled in agreement. "Mom couldn't have said no to extra hours for once?"

That was selfish, and Abby knew it, but they'd been plotting this trip to the zoo—and its world-class aviary—for months, ever since she got out of the hospital minus her appendix. It had seemed a miracle that her birthday fell on the zoo's annual free day. She only turned twelve once.

Einstein's claws pattered over her skin as he walked up her arm to nibble on her ear.

"Thanks, buddy, but ear nibbles aren't going to make me feel better today."

He kept nibbling anyway.

Abby sighed. She wandered into her mom's bedroom. There the window gave a clear view of their neighbor's birdfeeders.

"Black-capped chickadee," she whispered to Einstein as a perky black-and-white bird hopped down from a branch. It snagged a seed and flew away, its desire firmly secure in its beak.

"American goldfinch. House sparrow. Northern cardinal. Carolina wren." Each bird flitted in and out again, each one an arrow loosed into the sky, flying away from earthly cares and troubles. But none of them was the one—-the unidentified bird she'd been looking for since she saw it in the hospital.

Her mom insisted she'd hallucinated, insisted the bird was an effect of the anesthesia, a memory of a picture in a book. And Abby admitted it was unlikely she'd seen a black bird with teeth and claws in her hospital room. But she had seen it, plain as day, seen the way its feathers ruffled, its tail twitched, its black eyes gleamed as it peered out the window. If it had been a hallucination, it had looked just as real as the birds she saw every day.

And it didn't match anything she remembered seeing, or anything she'd seen since. It hadn't been a vulture or a crow. It hadn't been in any bird guide her mom brought home. She'd hoped she might see one at the zoo's aviary.

She sank down onto the folding chair her mom had angled so she could watch the birds. Something crinkled beneath her. She shot up, Einstein squawking on her shoulder in surprise.

A wrapped present lay on the chair. Her mom must have put it there knowing she'd come to this seat. She'd been so engrossed in the birds she hadn't seen it.

The wrapping paper had Tweety on it, of course. She ripped it open.

The book inside was square and thin, with a hard green cover. On the front was the drawing of a creature that made Abby gasp. It looked like a black chicken with teeth and a long tail.

"Einstein, that's the bird!"

She traced the title with her finger, sounding out the word: "Ar-kay-op-ter-ix." Then, faster. "Archaeopteryx."

The word sounded like a spell, something magical to be savored.

She flipped open the book, turning pages faster as she realized what she was reading. "Einstein, listen! You're descended from dinosaurs, and this was the very first dinosaur to become a bird. It had feathers and could fly and everything!"

Einstein peered down at the book from her shoulder, cocking his head as birds do, but Abby sat still, too excited to move. "The first bird, ever," she breathed.

Something soft fluttered in her chest. She rubbed her hand-me-down-jeans, wiggled her toes in her cousin's old sneakers.

What must it have been like to wear primordial feathers? To look to the high curtain of the sky and decide you would go there, no matter the obstacles?

"Fly, archaeopteryx, fly," she whispered. The book rested lightly on her knees, like a kiss or a prayer.

A dark blur winged past the window towards the feeders, but she kept her eyes on the book. One picture showed archaeopteryx on the ground, gazing at a high, high branch. She knew that feeling, that desperate desire to be somewhere, anywhere else.

She traced the picture with her finger. She had no idea why she might have seen an archaeopteryx in her hospital room, whether it had been a dream, a hallucination, or what. But she knew she'd never seen this book before, and she knew what she must do now. "I'm going to see one of these someday. For real."

Einstein chipped, a sound that could have been a protest. "I don't care if they've been extinct for millions of years." She held the book close. "Maybe it's impossible, but someday I'm going to see another archaeopteryx."

II. Semiplumes—small feathers that help make a bird insulated and aerodynamic, and that aid in courtship displays

Abby plunked herself down on the frat house picnic table. God, this party sucked even more than she'd thought it would. The music was bad, and the alcohol fumes were giving her a headache. She'd totally bail except she'd promised not to leave without her roommate, and Regan was across the yard sticking her tongue down some guy's throat.

Abby rolled her eyes. She snatched up an unused paper napkin from the table and rescued a pen from the trampled grass. A few sketch lines later, a giant archaeopteryx chomped the head off a stick figure frat boy.

She giggled and drew again. This time, she flew off into the sunset on the giant archaeopteryx's back, Regan gripped safely in its talons.

A guy's voice spoke at her shoulder. "What is the air-speed velocity of an unladen archaeopteryx?"

She quirked an eyebrow. How intriguing. Amid all the dumb jocks, someone could quote Monty Python. Without looking up, she said, "What do you mean? African or European archaeopteryx?"

"Ha! Archaeopteryx fossils have only been found in Europe."

"Very good." She looked up.

The guy at her shoulder wore baggy jeans and a t-shirt with the picture of a gray-and-yellow bird that she couldn't identify. His ears stuck out on both sides of his head, but rather than looking dopey he had a certain boy-next-door charm.

He stuck out his hand. "Luke Michaels."

Wow. He knew about archaeopteryx, had a bird on his shirt, could quote Monty Python, *and* was polite. It was a miracle. She shook. "Abby Weber. Were we in psychology together last year?" She thought she remembered his ears.

"Yup. You sat in front and asked lots of questions." "Well, Professor Kay wasn't clear on a lot of stuff."

"Agreed. I'd have asked those questions, but you beat me to them." He nodded at the picnic table. "Mind if I join you?" "Only if you tell me how you know about archaeopteryx."

He grinned. "I got my nerd credentials early. By the time I was six, I could name something like sixty different dinosaurs."

"That'll do." She scooted over so he could join her on the table. Across the yard, Regan didn't look like she was coming up for air anytime soon.

"How about you?" Luke asked as he settled in. "Why were you drawing an archaeopteryx of all things?"

Her vision was her own, not for other people. But a dinosaur-loving bird nerd might understand the resulting impossible dream. "I'm a biology major. I'm studying to be the first person to clone one."

Both his eyebrows rose. "You're gonna do a Jurassic Park?" "Except something the size of a blue jay won't eat me."

"Good point. When you get one cloned, can I take a picture?" He shrugged his shoulder, and Abby realized he had a camera slung over it.

"You're a photographer?" "Yup. Studio arts major." He plucked at the picture on his shirt. "I took this. It's a Kirtland's warbler."

No wonder she hadn't recognized the bird. Kirtland's warblers were critically endangered. "You saw one? How lucky!"

He beamed. "I'm gonna be a professional photographer, take pictures of things before they're gone, maybe help save them." He leaned close. He smelled not of alcohol, thank goodness, but soap and toothpaste. "What I really want is a picture of an ivory-billed woodpecker."

"They're probably extinct."

"Yeah." He hung his head. "That might be an impossible dream."

"Well, if I can clone an archaeopteryx, maybe I can clone an ivory-billed woodpecker, too."

"And I could take the pictures?" He pressed his hands to his heart, not mockingly, but in total sincerity. "It would be an honor."

Just like that, Abby knew this was the man she wanted to marry.

III. Body feathers—the colored feathers that help give a bird its identity

"I hate it," Abby said. Her voice was muffled by her face in her hands. "I'm listening to all the presentations, and these people are reporting their amazing work—getting clones to live for more than a week! Hatching chickens who display ancestral traits of teeth and bony tails! When I'm figuring out a better way to extract DNA from fossilized eggshells, and my boss won't let me publish yet. God, he's so paranoid." "Drink something." Luke pushed an orange juice across the restaurant table. "You'll feel better with some sugar in you."

Abby made a face but drank.

Out the restaurant window, Las Vegas simmered under the noontime sun. In the hotel hallway, people hurried past sporting green conference badges. Abby waved to one man, a scientist from Australia, before she downed another gulp.

"You're right." She plunked her glass down. "Sugar solves all. But I didn't ask how the photoshoot went. Did you get some good condor pictures?" "Fabulous! *National Geographic* should be thrilled with them. I wish you could've been there. This one condor—"

"Dr. Michaels?" A man in a grey suit with a blue tie approached the table. He carried a slim black briefcase but no conference badge. "Are you Abigail Michaels?" She straightened, aware of her rumpled t-shirt and jeans. "Probably. Who's asking?" The man extended a hand. "I'm Malcom Xavier. Is there a place we can speak privately?" Abby gestured to the table. "Here's fine. This is my husband, Luke. You can say anything you need to in front of him."

Mr. Xavier eyed Luke as if he regularly betrayed state secrets. Luke grinned, rubbing his unshaven chin for emphasis.

"All right," Mr. Xavier said. He slid into the booth, forcing Luke to scoot over.

Abby scooted over on her side so she faced Luke, not Mr. Xavier. "Well?" she asked. Whatever this guy had to say, it had better be good.

Mr. Xavier clasped his hands and rested his elbows on the table. "I represent Teddy Hardy."

"Who?"

Luke whistled. "The M-C-Squared.com guy? You know, we see his commercials all the time." "Exactly," Mr. Xavier said. "As you may guess, Mr. Hardy has an interest in science. In particular, in creatures long extinct."

Abby found herself straightening in her seat and smoothing her shirt. She wished she had bothered to put on mascara that morning. "Didn't he just give something like twenty million dollars to the Field Museum?" "Exactly," Mr. Xavier said. "Now Mr. Hardy wants to advance the field of de-extinction, to resurrect creatures no longer with us. He is prepared to build a lab for just such a purpose, and he's looking for someone to run the lab. Dr. Michaels, you're known to be a vocal proponent of de-extinction, and—"

"You're joking, right?" Abby looked from him to Luke, whose eyebrows seemed poised to hover over his head. "I haven't published in five years, didn't even present a poster session here. Other people"—she waved towards the Australian who had wandered into the bar—"are getting all sorts of publicity on their work to bring back the Tasmanian tiger, and..." She trailed off at Mr. Xavier's bemused expression. "No joke. Perhaps if you look at the contract you'll understand why I approached you." He slid a paper from his briefcase across the table. "You'll want to have your lawyer review it, of course." "Of course," Luke echoed. The closest they got to lawyers was watching them on TV.

Abby skimmed the paper. Her fingers began to tingle. "It says Mr. Hardy wants to focus on avifauna, bringing back extinct birds. Especially the first birds, the basal birds."

"Exactly. Mr. Hardy has learned of your work advancing DNA extraction from fossilized eggshells, as well of your interest in archaeopteryx." Abby clutched the table. It seemed her breathing had gone haywire. It wasn't surprising that someone from work had blabbed about her breakthroughs, and now—"You're offering me my own lab. To bring back an archaeopteryx."

Across the table, Mr. Xavier dipped his chin. "Exactly." Luke craned his neck, reading the contract upside down. "The lab would be in New York City? But you're only offering a starting salary of $50,000."

"Most of the startup money will be invested in equipment, you understand. But we offer a generous benefits package."

"Oh," Abby said, her heart sinking. Not only was Mr. Hardy interested in her science, but he knew that without recent publications to her name, he could get her cheap. "But, Luke, we talked about me finding a position that would let you open your own gallery."

"We both know that'll take years. Impossible dreams start from humble beginnings, remember? I'll make great contacts in the city, and we'll be an easy driving distance to lots of places. I've always wanted to photograph piping plovers on Cape Cod."

"You have? You never said."

He pressed his hands to his heart. "This is a fabulous chance for you. Take it."

"You're sure?"

"I'm counting the days to my first archaeopteryx picture."

She took a breath, afraid her heart would shoot into her throat. The signature line on the contract stood out bold as an airplane's runway. She rummaged in her bag for a pen.

IV. Bristles—stiff feathers that help protect a bird's eyes and beak

"The lab door was *padlocked*?" Luke demanded. Abby had never seen him so angry.

"And a note on the door said all the equipment's to be repossessed!" She stomped through the gray slush. A gray sky spit gray snow onto the gray New York sidewalk. "God, six years of work, gone."

Luke scowled at the passing traffic. "I mean, we knew Mr. Hardy was having money problems, but to just close the lab like that...is there anything you can do?"

"I called that lawyer your brother recommended, but probably not." She kicked a discarded soda can. "I mean, the eggshell DNA hadn't panned out, and we never were able to get DNA from those fossilized embryos. But I would have thought of something else. I would have!" She bit her lip.

"Christ." Luke jammed his hands into his pockets. It'd been years since she'd heard him swear.

A car alarm blared, the noise grating like claws against her ears. As abruptly, it stopped.

"Hey," Luke said, his voice brighter. "Come with me to Europe."

"What? Now?"

"In two weeks, my trip for *Scientific American*."

"When you're shooting the Białowieża?" It was one of the largest tracks of intact primeval forest left in Europe, home to rare and endangered animals.

"Yup. We could extend the trip, go to Germany, maybe—"

"Visit the museums? See the archaeopteryx specimens?"

"Yup." He grinned.

"Oh, yes!" She stopped, threw her arms around him. She'd seen the fossils before, of course, but years ago. It wasn't the same as a real thing, but..."A little pick me up is exactly—"

Tires screeched. Abby turned.

A bus careened up over the sidewalk. The driver's panicked eyes stared down at her. Then all went black.

V. Retrices—tail feathers used to steer and brake in flight

"Again," Luke said.

"I'm trying," Abby snapped. She knew she sounded peevish, but no matter what she did her stupid fingers wouldn't stretch the rubber band looped around them.

"Okay, I'll get the ball the therapist gave you. Maybe that'll work better." Luke grabbed his crutches and limped out of the kitchen, favoring his fractured ankle.

Abby slumped in her chair, cradling her ruined right hand. She should be grateful to be alive. If she hadn't stopped to hug Luke, if the two of them had been one step closer to the curb, the bus would've done worse than sideswipe them. But gratitude was hard when she couldn't hold a pen, let alone a test tube or an eye dropper.

She flexed her hand, but nope. Her fingers barely moved.

With a shake of her head, she looked up from the ruins of her arm. On the table lay stills from the project she was working on with one of Luke's friends. The man was making a film about the origins of birds. She'd thrown herself into her role as scientific advisor, desperate to keep her mind occupied while her body healed. But no matter how she tried, the project couldn't calm her impossible cravings. The animations were good, very good, but the archaeopteryx portrayed there wasn't living. There was no mind, no beating heart behind the images.

A blur at her window startled her. She leaned, searching for what headed towards their feeders. Instead, she saw a dinosaur hopping up and down in the courtyard.

Not a real dinosaur, no, rather someone in one of those T-Rex costumes. She'd seen videos of them, ice-skating, chasing jeeps, frightening small dogs. This one was followed by a second, smaller T-Rex, and she recognized their neighbor's two sons. The boys had asked her more than once to tell them about archaeopteryx and had hung on to her every word. No wonder their mom had gotten them costumes.

She pressed her cheek to the glass, watching the boys chase each other in the courtyard, their tails bobbing, their arms flailing in the ridiculous costumes. How lively, how joyous they looked.

The smaller boy stumbled. His foot hit the corner of a planter, and he slammed snout-first onto the pavement.

Abby sucked in her breath. Was he all right? Should she call his mom?

She reached for her phone, but the boy righted himself, laughing with the easy resiliency of the young.

As he did, he must have seen her in the window. He waved, his movements endearingly awkward in the costume.

She waved with her good arm and realized she was grinning. As silly as the costumes looked, as awkward and make-believe as they were, the very gracelessness warmed her heart. Here were living, breathing creatures beneath the images.

Behind her, Luke gasped. "Abby, whatever you just did, do it again."

Around her damaged fingers, the rubber band stretched taut.

VI. Secondaries—a bird's wing feathers, which provide lift in flight

A shriek of laughter brought Abby to the activity room door. She peeked out into the main hall of the Michaels Science Center. There, families worked their way through hands-on exhibits about everything from photography to Earth's vanishing species to the evolution of birds. One little girl in particular couldn't seem to get enough of the ride-on archaeopteryx. Her black pig-tails bounced in time with its feathers.

"This is what I'm going to make," her older sister said, tapping the archaeopteryx's head. "I'm going to be the first person to clone one."

"Me, too!" black pigtails said. "I'll clone one."

"You can be the second person."

"Deal."

They pinky swore, and Abby ducked back inside the activity room, grinning.

Still smiling, she hung a piñata from the activity room ceiling. The Center was hosting another birthday party that after-noon, and she wanted everything to be ready before she left. Whistling, she strung dinosaur lights on the walls and set out plastic dinosaur plates on the cake table. Their kid-sized T-Rex costume she'd carefully folded in one corner. Amira, their assis-tant, would help the birthday boy inside before he took the first swing at the piñata.

The staff door opened. "Abs," Luke called, "it's time."

"Coming." She stepped back from the cake table. The Center had been their brainchild in the year after The Accident, when they decided they needed jobs where they could work side-by-side, where it didn't matter if Abby's hand shook or Luke's ankle throbbed. Now, as she cast a critical eye over the room, she took a deep breath, let it out. The room looked perfect. The Center was a success. She'd married a wonderful man and brought science to thousands of children. One of them, she was sure, would hold a living archaeopteryx in their hands.

She carried the satisfaction close as Luke opened the car door for her and made sure she was safely inside.

I'm not made of glass, she wanted to protest, but she held her tongue. He needed something to do in face of her illness.

At the hospital, nurses whisked her into a surgical gown. It was stiff and harsh against her skin, chafing at the neck. Once she was prepped and on the gurney, they ushered Luke in.

He gripped her hand. "I'll be waiting right outside."

Abby gripped back. Dormant fears wormed through her belly. What if something went wrong with the surgery? What if the surgeon found that her cancer had spread? "I know," she said and forced a smile. "See you soon."

"It's time," the nurse said.

Luke leaned over and kissed her. She held his hand as long as she could. As she let go, she saw it.

A plastic archaeopteryx stood on the shelf over her gurney. Probably a left-behind toy, it seemed to carry in its plastic wings all the comfort of an icon on an altar, all the assurances of her own guardian angel. What serendipity. She gasped.

"What?" Luke asked, his gaze never leaving her face.

"Archaeopteryx," she whispered.

He turned. At the sight of the toy, his shoulders lifted.

"It's going to be okay," she said, and as they wheeled her away, she realized it was true. She didn't know why archaeopteryx had come into her life, would never know why this longing had been hers to carry, but whatever happened next, she had Luke and the

Center waiting. Because of archaeopteryx. It was all she could ask for from an impossible dream.

"Fly, archaeopteryx, fly," she whispered as the anesthesia took over.

Mouse, Crow, Cockroach, Valkyrie

Tiffany Meuret

Tiffany is a writer and poet hailing from
Phoenix, Arizona. Her debut, A Flood
of Posies, releases in September 2020
with Black Spot Books. Find her online
atwww.TiffanyMeuret.com or Twitter
@TMeuretBooks for an unlimited
supply of dog pictures.

A foul stench had permeated the air for days. Even down in her little burrow with her little pups, the sourness of it chased her. Mama Mouse had lived in this particular hole for many generations of offspring, and this new scent was enough to keep her senses alert throughout the dark periods in which she usually rested.

It was hot and acrid and dusty this time of year, and her babies were too small yet to leave. So she left them unattended for an afternoon to forage, steering clear of the new greenness that had sprung to life as suddenly as a single dark, that swiftly filled the large expanse of dead dirt space between her quaint burrow and the sharpness the tall animals had built. Something about the greens rankled the fur on her back, and she avoided them as she would the snakes that wriggled their way into her burrow on occasion, seeking out her helpless babies to consume. These greens were fast, like predators, and Mama knew better than to trust them.

She was farther away than she'd have liked when the sour scent changed. A breeze picked it up, lifting it over the untended desert, across the long blackness the tall animals laid down for their screaming shiny monsters, towards Mama who hovered in the shadows looking for critters and seeds in the dirt. It was the smell of death. Mama knew it better than most.

It was those greens. Those things that should be food but instead brought a foulness that senses only as keen as her own could detect. The tall animals, as miraculous as they could be, were dumb to these things. Still, Mama raced back, propelled by an instinct to protect her young, knowing they were already dead, yet going anyway.

Inside her burrow, tucked so reliably in a blank space of land the tall animals rarely traversed, in a place meant to be secure, laid her lifeless pups, strangled by a noxious odor that wet the eyes with pain. Mama had hardly the time to glance at them before retreating, another primal sense moving her paws beyond her grief.

Her burrow was lost. Everything in it, lost. Mama gazed from a safe space some distance away at the sharpness that had shielded her burrow for so long. Tall animals lived inside it, all in matching skins that they made. Mama observed the dead walking and talking and moving in their matching skins, oblivious to it all. All animals knew death, though some seemed to like it more than others, despite its ruthlessness to all things alive.

Above, something that might like to eat her *cawed*, circling. Mama scattered, claws scratching the foul breeze that chased her, leaving the tall animals to their inevitable end.

***

Crow considered the mouse below simply due to the speed of its movement, then forgot about it. Far more interesting things were afoot. Crow noticed the minute yet continual wriggling of the strange plants below—wriggling of plants that did not belong.

At first, Crow thought these were just another construction of humans, considering their reckless ambition to interfere with anything their hands could touch, but these plants were too precise. In a matter of days they had not only sprouted small buds from the Earth up, but begun emitting the most obnoxious odor Crow had ever encountered. She would only cross them from the safety of a high tailwind, sailing over them from a safe distance.

The intrusion initially irritated Crow. This was her favorite place to perch, watching the humans in their cages. These humans decorated themselves in the same bright colors, shuffling about in lines, sometimes bound by the hands or feet, and sometimes free to run about but only in contained areas. The bright humans were smaller than the rest, too, which Crow appreciated. Of the ones inside the caged area, the smaller humans were generally more agreeable to creatures like her than the big ones, who were drab in color and rather prickly most of the time. Crow made sure to perch in areas that only the little ones looked toward, and her gamble was sometimes rewarded with crumbs and other unwanted trinkets the humans tossed at her. Her favorites were the shiny silver wrappers, but the little ones weren't always keen to give them up, though it seemed to please them when she stole away with whatever they'd discarded.

So the encroachment of this new plant left her excitable and tired, having circled above it for a few days now, only landing to sleep and pick off scattering rodents that too seemed to sense doom on the wind. And for the hustle and sprinting and circling, the humans seemed to have not noticed. Crow hadn't landed inside the cages for two days now. A few of the small ones tried to lure her down, but she refused. A big human rode out into the field with one of its machines, prodding the plants with his feet and hands, only to retreat inside again without a bother. It surprised her, yet then again these humans were more adept than most at manipulating intolerant conditions. Where Crow would take flight for better lands, humans bent the lands to their will. Crow admired their dominance, no matter how tenuous.

It wasn't until another night had passed and the plants had crept up to the cage walls, snaking their tendrils in tight loops through the shiny grey of it, smothering the sharpness of it, that the alarms inside the human cages set the air alight. Crow launched from her perch (a tree with green bark far enough away that the odor didn't sting) with terror. She knew the sound, having heard it before on multiple occasions. The cages screamed and screamed like an animal, and only seemed to do so when there was trouble.

The humans had finally sensed the danger. Far too late, Crow suspected, to do anything about it. Though they had surprised her before.

Flying overhead, the big humans scrambled back and forth within the cages. Many more than Crow had ever seen in one place within these confines. All of them traveled in the same direction, towards one area in particular, disappearing inside one of the buildings in which the little ones lived. Crow needn't get any closer to understand why—panic was universal, and she, a crow, had a particular knack of sensing it. Being a scavenger made her acutely aware of death's tangy aroma from very far distances.

In and out, in and out again. They looked like startled cats from this distance, but the humans were not what held her fast attention. The plants were moving again, this time with more visible strength and purpose. Vines scaled the cages and crept snake-like through the enclosure with a swiftness only an animal with wings could escape, and though Crow's interest was now piqued beyond measure, she dare not land anywhere near these things. She wasn't even sure how long it would be safe to fly above them, whatever the distance. These weren't like any plants she'd even seen before, and while her curious urge was overwhelming, nothing could overpower her will to survive.

After a few more circles above the cages, Crow flew off while her energy still maintained, moving furiously upwind of the poisonous breeze, screaming alarm to any creature with sense enough to heed it.

***

Nothing was heeded, to the delight of the cockroaches. The plants took everything, snuffed out life within a mile radius in a matter of weeks. But roaches are survivors, and as such made a habit of seeking refuge in destruction, certain they would come out of it just fine. As it turned out, this juvenile detention center, recently abandoned of life, was prime real estate and they were not a species to waste a good opportunity when they found it.

They crawled in and out of rotting eye sockets, slacked jaws hanging from rotting tendon and muscle, barely clinging to the skull that used to support them. They crawled through the bars of the jail cells to the bodies, crawled on the concrete floors to the bodies, crawled up the walls and along the bones of bodies forever frozen by the grip of vines. They crawled through the withering stomach cavities of bodies and over the pile of bodies that had locked themselves in a small room, toppled on top of one another as they died, their guns splattered just out of reach. They crawled through the holes of those that had been shot, through the choked and the strangled. They crawled through the degraded flesh, no longer supple and ripe, but a soupy muck that stuck the remains to their graves like cement.

Outside the facility, their brethren crawled through homes once fortified—the people gone, their animals nothing but bones inside the droppings of other larger things, likely decomposing somewhere else.

The plants wouldn't have registered at all with the roaches, if not for the smorgasbord they brought along with them. That, and the silence. Cockroaches were attuned to the hustle and bustle of life—they thrived in the heavy clomping of existence, slipping in and out of shadows and cracks, running up walls and in the crevices other things refused to travel. It was a good life, very good indeed, but this was exquisite.

It had been quiet for weeks. Many weeks. The plants arrived in a flash, killed in a flash, spreading and spreading until those that stayed behind were consumed and those that stayed alive had long fled. At first the humans screamed, then they roared, then they built tall walls to keep the plants at bay, ones that lurched high and menacing, walls that trapped the people inside so that they could not run away. They died, and the silence came. It was then that the roaches flooded toward the area, the quiet snaking its way to them like dinner bell tinnitus.

The roaches arrived, nothing to stop them.

And the plants heaved and belched, swelling in spots that writhed as the roaches traversed the thorny vines that connected them. This ground was a poisonous fertilizer, growing nothing but pain and sorrow, and the plants responded in kind. And roaches crawled and ate, ate and crawled, crawled and ate, until one day when the plants awoke.

It was that day, many weeks since, that the ground began to make noise. It began to move. Something unearthly that had taken shelter there, beginning its fetal squirm. And the cock-roaches, being the survivors that they are, knew right then that it was time to get the fuck out of dodge. The buffet had closed, the food picked clean, and the ground under their feet was growing angrier by the moment.

It was only then that anyone should have been afraid, for to see the cockroaches run was to witness an event that nothing—not even they—could survive.

***

Precious life is often born from dark places, and this is no different. The plants had done their duty, drilling through upward through the earth, pungent with the sulfurous place of their birth. They wended and broke at the weakest point—a place so thin it could have cracked with a whimper.

These vines were the hems of the Valkyries, the angels, the sirens, creatures with many names. These thorns built their swords, the roots their armor, the ropey stalks their eyes and their voices that rubbed together in whispers.

The Earth cracked away under the force of their might, their bodies upheaved, dragging the corpses of the dead with them into the sky, placing kisses on the cold cheeks of the innocents before sending them to their final place of rest—a place the Valkyries did not know and could not predict. The rest fell carelessly into the abyss, bones splintered in the descent.

The unstoppable force of the plants, sprouting from nowhere and obliterating any and all detractors, had now birthed a plague. The Valkyries, birthed of blood and marrow and rust and sorrow and dirt and consideration, had finally wretched free of their shells. They were topside. They were tired, thrilled, stealing heavy, venomous breaths before charging forward in the same methodical, careful manner as their creation.

The Valkyries laughed at the paltry walls meant to keep them, then screamed a song that cracked new places in the Earth, more stealthy green buds ready to emerge into the sun.

And the world could do nothing, but watch them come.

What the Gods Left Behind

Genevieve Gornichec

Genevieve Gornichec earned her degree in History, but she got as close to majoring in Vikings as she possibly could. Her debut novel, THE WITCH'S HEART, releases in early 2021. Originally from Cleveland, Ohio, she now lives even deeper in the Midwest and can be found on Twitter at @ironwitchy.

Katla was on the verge of collapse when she spotted the farmhouse.

She could pitch her tent anywhere, so it wasn't a matter of seeking shelter before nightfall. It was the potential of finding provisions—anything that hadn't been picked over by the nine years of scavengers before her—that made her keep moving even as dusk descended and every muscle screamed at her to rest.

She was so tired of walking. And according to the ancient, crumbling road map she'd been using to follow the interstates north, she was only at her halfway point: Nebraska.

Her stomach sank as she drew closer to the house. It was clear that she wasn't going to have much luck here; the door was hanging from the top hinge, vines snaking through every shattered window and up the peeling blue siding. The front yard was as untidy as the miles and miles of overgrown cornfields surrounding it, and in the backyard stood an equally decrepit barn with a single, enormous oak tree looming over its sagging roof.

It never ceases to amaze me how quickly nature takes over. She pushed her glasses up her nose and tromped up the dusty driveway, adjusting the enormous camping pack on her shoulders. It's been less than ten years, and soon it will be like we were never here at all.

She stepped onto the creaking front porch and moved the door aside, the single rusty hinge shrieking in protest, the heady smell of decay hitting her as soon as she crossed the threshold. The interior of the house was dense with moss, and ivy had pushed through the soggy wooden window frames. But as far as she could tell, there were no bodies. The place was empty save for the overturned furniture and several rodents' nests, the latter of which were in plain sight.

The animals were much bolder now than they were before the Collapse. Not even mice were afraid anymore.

Katla was surprised that nothing bigger had taken over the house by now. Predators were the least of her worries these days, for prey abounded and she wasn't worth the trouble by comparison. Nevertheless, she pulled her flashlight from the side pocket of her pack and headed for the kitchen. She found the pantry bare save for a small can of beans tucked into the back corner.

She immediately put the flashlight down and snatched up the camping tool from her belt, opened the can, and wolfed down the beans using the blade of her knife; when they were gone, her stomach growled for more. Most days she was so far beyond hunger that she didn't even feel it. But she knew she needed to keep up her strength, even though any little bit of food made the emptiness unbearable for a while before it subsided again.

She shuffled out of the pantry and glanced through the busted kitchen window. The sun had nearly disappeared; it was time to pitch her tent. Katla had sworn to herself when this all began that she'd never stay in abandoned houses, for they contained the two things she hoped most to avoid: ghosts, and the bodies they left behind.

Ghosts, because the fact that she could see them was proof she was going mad. Bodies, because they could kill her.

As she headed for the front door, she heard a small voice say from behind her, "Um, ma'am? You should check the treehouse."

Katla's shoulders stiffened and she hung her head, but she didn't turn around.

"Ma'am, did you hear me?" The voice sounded like a child's, and Katla winced. It was so much harder when they were young.

"I heard you," Katla mumbled, and turned.

The child couldn't have been more than five or six when he passed, and he had the same hollow-eyed look as the rest of them—or at least she thought he did, before his eyebrows shot up beneath his bowl cut and he gave her a hopeful grin. His two front teeth were missing.

Katla felt a pang in her chest.

"There's food up there, ma'am." He moved toward her with an eerie grace, the outlines of his body drifting like wisps of smoke, and gestured with a small hand. "Come on, I'll show you."

She had no choice but to follow him out to the massive old oak in the backyard. The treehouse was almost entirely hidden by the branches and the ivy that wound its way up the tree's immense trunk, hiding the rotting wooden ladder that led up to the platform.

As the child led them across the yard, Katla stopped short when she saw a dog leering at her from the tall grass between her and the tree. She'd grown wary of wild dogs on her journey—many had turned vicious with starvation—but this one she recognized.

This dog had been following her since Kansas City despite her best attempts to lose it. And it talked, which to Katla was more worrying than her suddenly being able to see ghosts.

"You," she hissed. "Get lost, mutt."

The dog looked smug. Gravel dust from the road coated its scraggly gray fur and pointed ears; one eye was a piercing blue, the other clouded and milky as if it belonged not to the creature but to some more ancient thing.

You can't get rid of me that easily, Katla Brynjólfsdóttir, it said.

Katla started, for she'd never told the dog her name—any of them. She'd grown so used to being Kat Dawes here in America that hearing her given name pronounced correctly—along with her patronymic—gave her pause.

It's official, she thought. I'm going mad.

"He looks like a good boy," said the ghost-child. "Or...girl? I can't tell."

"Boy," said Katla, for the timbre of the dog's voice in her head was distinctly male. The problem was, of course, that it had a voice in the first place.

"Leave me alone," Katla snapped, stomping forward menacingly in an attempt to scare it off. But the dog didn't move, so she stared it down as she headed past it and toward the tree, placing a tentative boot on the bottom rung of the wooden ladder against the trunk. It seemed a solid foothold, so she made her way up carefully, step by step, testing her weight—and that of the camping pack strapped to her back—to make sure the decomposing wood wouldn't crumble beneath her feet.

The ghost-child had followed her through the grass and now observed her ascent, looking wounded. "I'm just trying to help."

"I wasn't talking to you, kid," Katla grunted as she climbed. A few of the rungs buckled beneath her weight, so she moved faster. Only a few feet to go.

"Who were you talking to, then?" the ghost-child called up to her with a sideways glance at the dog, who now of course wore the blank stare of a normal, witless animal.

Katla heaved herself up onto the platform and crawled into the treehouse. Once she pulled herself to a sitting position, she unclasped the pack's straps from the front of her chest before flinging it off her shoulders and sagging with relief.

Fumbling for her flashlight in the gloom, she craned her head over the edge of the platform and saw the dog plop itself down at the base of the ladder. It stared up at her with patient disinterest, like it had all the time in the world and nothing better to do.

"You're a creep," she muttered, then yelped when she turned and saw that the ghost child had suddenly appeared in the corner. His body gave off a soft ethereal glow, which brightened with worry as Katla nearly dropped her flashlight.

"Sorry, I didn't mean to frighten you!" he cried, holding up his hands.

"It's all right," Katla said, regaining her composure. Before she shone the flashlight anywhere else, she said cautiously, "Your body isn't up here, is it?" The remains of Plague victims were still contagious long after the affliction had taken their lives. And if the Plague had taken him...

"No." He gave a nod toward the house. "It's in my bedroom."

Katla studied him. "Your parents just left it there?"

The child lowered his hands and looked away. "They left me here. When I got sick, they went for help, and they—they never came back. Not even after I was gone."

"I see." Her skin prickled with goosebumps. The Plague, then. It must've been in the early days. Back when we thought there was a cure.

Either that, or his parents had already known there was no hope and had no choice but to leave the child to die rather than risk catching the sickness themselves.

"Before the lights went out, they were saying on my daddy's radio show that the world was coming to an end," the child said, as if reading her thoughts. "Daddy has been collecting cans and water jugs since before I was born." He deflated. "The looters took everything from the cellar."

Katla felt a twinge more sympathy for the child's parents. If they'd left all their supplies behind, they had probably meant to return.

Any number of things could have prevented them from doing so.

"But," the child added, mistaking her expression for disappointment about the food situation, "I hid some of it up here before I got real sick."

He scooted to the opposite corner, where a blue plastic tarp covered a lumpy pile the size of a small child. Katla was glad that they'd already established that his body wasn't in the treehouse. She went to lift the tarp, careful not to touch the ghost-child's form—for, as she'd learned the hard way, she very much could—and gasped.

"This is incredible," she whispered. Tears pricked her eyes as she took it all in, her flashlight trembling in her hand. Along with water filters and several cans of soups she hadn't tasted since before the Collapse, there were also at least a dozen boxes of protein bars stuffed into clear plastic bins to keep them safe from rodents and raccoons.

She waited another long moment before asking, "How can I ever repay you?"

"Well, since you mentioned it, ma'am..." The child leaned back against the wall. "I wonder if before you go, could you—could you bury me?"

Katla froze.

"We buried Grandpop even when we couldn't afford it because Mommy said if he didn't have a proper Christian burial he wouldn't go to Heaven," the child continued, a tremor in his voice. "So if it isn't too much trouble...?"

Katla didn't believe that burying a body in the ground had anything to do with Heaven, but then again, she didn't know for sure. *What if I say no and I end up being the reason this kid never sees his family again?*

"Of course," she whispered as she replaced the tarp with reverence. She would sort through the food and deal with the consequences of her promise tomorrow. "It's no trouble at all. I'll do it first thing in the morning, and then I'll need to be on my way."

Even as the words left her lips, a chill ran through her at the thought of being so close to a Plague-stricken body. At the needless danger she was putting herself in, just to help a stranger maybe get where he was supposed to go.

"Where are you headed, anyway?" he asked as she unrolled her sleeping bag. The treehouse was spacious enough for even a woman as tall as Katla to spread out comfortably.

"My mother's cabin near Lake Winnipeg. Just outside the town of Gimli."

"Where'd you come from?"

"Houston area."

"But that's a long way, ma'am! Can't you drive?"

Katla grimaced. She'd set out in her SUV, but found it attracted too much attention from scavenger gangs and gas was hard to come by, so she'd abandoned it before she'd even made it out of Texas.

She felt safer on foot, anyway.

"Not really," she said. "Too dangerous."

"Oh. Is your mom expecting you?"

Katla zipped the sleeping bag around her and rested her head on her grimy pack. Closed her eyes. Told herself for the millionth time that she wasn't crazy, that she wasn't on a fool's errand, that this was all a bad dream and she would wake up and it would be ten years ago and she'd be snuggled up in her bed with her husband and daughter and the world would be as it was before the floods and the famines. Before the wars and the Plague. Before the last space shuttles left, never to return.

Before she was more or less the last woman on Earth.

"Yes," Katla said finally, though her mother was almost certainly dead. "I believe she is."

***

Katla no longer dreamed, and that night—as every night—she thought of her mother and father, and her husband and Brynn.

She was ten when her parents took her and left Iceland, just as their peers in the scientific community started focusing all their attention inward. Iceland was on its way to total self-sufficiency well before the first signs of the Collapse, and efforts only doubled to insulate the island once all the signs pointed toward imminent doom.

Iceland might even still exist, though Katla had no way of knowing.

Her parents disagreed with their colleagues' attitudes and moved to the States, where they felt they could make a difference. They wanted to share what they knew, even though the world wouldn't listen, hadn't listened for decades. They believed the fate of all mankind was tied to their work.

They were right, but they paid dearly for it.

Just after Katla married Peter and moved with him to his home in Texas, her father died in one of the first floods—died believing there was still hope for humanity, even as those who could afford it boarded shuttles and fled for the safety of outer space—and then, just before Brynn was born, Katla's mother gave up and retired to their summer cabin in Manitoba, where the climate was just a little more temperate than the scorching, cloying heat of the American South.

Then the rest of the ice caps melted and the crops failed and the wars broke out, and the Plague hit the remaining land masses as the icing on the metaphorical cake.

Katla had not heard from her mother since before the lights went out.

Not directly, anyway.

More than half the world had perished by that point. Peter had already died in the wars, and Katla and her daughter had done what they could to survive in their home in the countryside, where they banded together with their neighbors and helped each other defend against the wildfires and the tide of hungry, sick people fleeing Houston's floods.

Then the last wave of the Plague passed through their small town, and it took Brynn with it.

Katla didn't leave her bed for weeks after that. In her absence, the rest of the town either died or realized they had to move on, and she was nearly dead herself when Brynn's ghost came to her, kneeling at the edge of the bed.

"You have to go, Mamma," the girl's spirit said softly. "You'll die if you stay here. Amma says to go to Gimli. She says to find her there."

She remembered reaching for Brynn in disbelief, expecting her hand to pass right through the girl's shoulder—but then her fingers touched Brynn's ghost as though it were cold and solid, and Katla's eyes widened in horror.

At her touch, her daughter's form brightened, shifted, then began to break apart. She remembered the look of relief on Brynn's face as she disappeared, but again it was Katla's own fault she was gone.

"No, no!" Katla sobbed, sitting upright, grasping for anything that remained of her daughter's ghost. "Brynn, come back! Brynn!"

After, she cried until she couldn't move. Then she dragged herself out of bed, forced down some food and let it settle, and remembered her daughter's words, Brynn's message from a grandmother she'd never even met.

Brynn says to go to Gimli.

So Katla went.

***

"I'm sorry to wake you, ma'am, but is that a book?"

Katla wormed her arms up through her tight sleeping bag and nudged her glasses aside to rub her eyes. The ghost-child was pointing to her half-open camping pack, where the worn corner of her daughter's favorite picture book was just visible in the bright moonlight.

"Mmm, yeah, it's a book," Katla said, sitting up and adjusting her glasses. They were never far from her, since she'd never get another pair. She wished now more than ever that she'd gotten laser eye surgery while she still could.

"They stopped making those before I was born," the child said.

"It's from when my mom was a kid." Katla pulled the book out and held it in her lap, ran a callused hand over the worn cover. "She passed it down to me, and I passed it down to my daughter. It was her favorite. My kid's, I mean. My mom's, too, I guess."

She leaned heavily against the wall, drawing her knees up and resting the book atop her thighs and grubby shorts as the child crept from the corner and sat down on the sleeping bag next to her. The first sunbeams sneaking in from the eastern window cast his spectral form in an eerie orange glow.

"What's it called?" he asked, staring blankly at the words on the cover.

"This—it's a book from my homeland, across the ocean. A book of Norse myths."

"Myths," the boy echoed, confused.

"Yep. They're very old stories about the gods and goddesses that people used to believe in." People like my parents. Her father, the climatologist who'd lit candles and made offerings to Odin and Thor and Frey; her mother, the biochemist who'd left out offerings for the land spirits. "Would you like me to read them to you?"

The boy nodded. Katla had to wonder if he had any concept at all of what she was talking about, but he asked no more questions, so Katla cracked open the dusty spine and began. The book contained simple retellings of the myths, the crude and gruesome bits—all the good parts, all the important parts—cleaned up and packaged nicely for children. She gestured at the illustrations as she read the stories of the Nine Worlds, of the gods: one-eyed Odin and his magic spear and his many names; beautiful Freyja and her golden necklace and her falcon cloak; and cunning Loki, mighty Thor, and all the rest.

She read all the way up to Ragnarök, their end. The sun had almost risen by then.

"Rag-na-rook?" the boy repeated after her, frowning. "It almost sounds like what happened to us, doesn't it? To our world?"

Katla said nothing. She'd read the book so many times that she could see the illustration in her mind before she turned the page. It showed the young gods, the ones who'd survived Ragnarök, pulling their ancestors' possessions from the ashes as the world renewed around them, green and thriving where the gods' halls in Asgard once stood.

Through the window Katla caught a glimpse of something shooting across the brightening sky: the tiny speck of Space Station Earth, containing some of the world's brightest scientists, but also those who had the money to buy salvation. The ones whose wealth and power had caused all of this in the first place, saved; the rest of humanity, the victims of their greed, left behind to die.

The last thing Katla heard before the lights went out was that the scientists aboard the station were eventually planning to terraform and colonize Mars, a rumor that had been going around for years before the Collapse. Except now, instead of being the hope of all mankind, Mars would be a planet inhabited only by the rich and the super-intelligent.

I wonder if they'll come back one day and dig up what's left of us, she thought darkly. I wonder if we'll be artifacts in a Martian museum.

"Gosh." The ghost-child ran his hand over the illustration of Thor's redheaded twins unearthing his famous hammer, Mjölnir. His fingers were dangerously close to brushing her hand.

Katla twitched away from him and closed the book. Stuffed it back in her pack. Zipped up her sleeping bag. All without looking at him.

"I need to get moving," she said. The ghost-child watched wordlessly as she ripped aside the tarp and stuffed as much of the food as she possibly could into her pack. The rest of it she wrapped up in the tarp itself, which she lowered from the platform with a rope, sharp eyes scanning the farm for other scavengers.

No sign of the one-eyed dog. Good.

Katla took out another rope and lowered her pack next. She knew that the rotting ladder had been ready to give out on her way up, and she worried that the new weight of the bulging pack might be too much if attached to her person.

Her supplies safely on the ground, Katla turned and carefully picked her way down the ladder, praying it would hold. Before the Collapse she hadn't exactly been a small woman—her love of sweets, her desk job in accounting, and the birth of her daughter had seen to that—but by the time she'd left Houston after years of surviving on the town's small rations, which had quickly turned to fending for herself and Brynn, all of Katla's clothes had been too large and unbearable in the heat. She'd been fortunate enough to scavenge new shorts from a half-wrecked sporting goods store on her journey, and a new pair of hiking boots since the pair she'd left Texas with had been almost worn through by that point.

At least I'll never need winter clothes again, she thought grimly as she descended. Even in February in Manitoba. Nowhere in the world has winter anymore.

She was thankful for the new boots. They helped her keep her footing now. Just a little further and—

Crack.

The next thing Katla knew she was falling, and then her tailbone exploded in pain. She swore in several different languages before she heard a chuckle from the grass to her right and turned to see the one-eyed dog watching, amused.

I'm surprised you made it down in one piece, it said.

"Shut up," Katla sneered, tossing her thin, grimy blonde braid over her shoulder as she struggled to her feet. "How many times do I have to ask you to leave me alone?"

At least once more, the dog replied seriously.

As if on cue, a sparrow appeared from nowhere and attempted to sink its tiny talons into the dog's muzzle, flapping and chirping with annoyance. The dog made an irritated sound and shook its head as if shaking off a fly, and the sparrow subsided and landed on the hound's back.

Will you stop heckling the girl? said the sparrow haughtily, in a woman's voice. The dog turned over its shoulder and leered, but the sparrow remained unruffled. She's come this far. Leave the child be.

Katla blinked. She guessed that by now she was closer to forty than thirty, and anyway did not remember the last time she was called "child." Besides, the bird looked vaguely familiar, and its eyes were an unnatural golden color.

"Look, I don't know who you two are, but I need you to fuck off," she said to them. "I've got enough to worry about without hearing animals' voices in my head."

Before either could say another word, Katla turned to the ghost-child—who had appeared on her left—and said, "Sorry. Don't say the f-word."

The spirit seemed concerned. "Ma'am, who...were you talking to?"

Instead of trying to deny it, Katla's shoulders sagged and she gestured vaguely to her right. "Just that mutt and his bird friend. Don't worry about it."

The child looked past her to the now-empty spot of grass. His brow furrowed.

Katla followed his gaze and saw that her irksome companions had disappeared, and she sighed.

"All right, kid. Where do you want to be buried?"

***

He chose the shadow of the oak tree.

Katla grabbed a shovel from the empty barn and dug for most of the morning. Then she allowed herself to be escorted upstairs to a room at the end of the hall, where the boy gestured silently at the skeletal corpse on the bed, which cemented Katla's initial assumption that he was one of the Plague's first victims.

She pulled the collar of her tank top over her nose and entered the room, wishing she had a mask and gloves as she gathered the bedsheets around the remains. Rumors had gone around that touch was the way to transmit the Plague; still others had said that it was airborne. What she knew for sure was that it could incubate on any piece of flesh still attached to a body, waiting for another host.

Damn you and your conscience, Kat, Peter would say if he were there. *Just get that kid in the ground as quickly as you can. You need to learn how to say no.*

It was nearly noon when the body was buried and the hole filled, and Katla set the last stone on the cairn she'd piled atop the grave.

"Thank you," said the ghost-child. He closed his eyes and stood beside her for a moment as if waiting for something to happen. Katla knew exactly what, and stood beside him in silence.

I did the right thing, she told herself. He and his supplies have saved my life, so I gave a dead boy his last wish.

Several minutes passed before he opened his eyes and cast them down at the cairn. He could barely manage the words, "Why am I still here?"

Kat pulled on her pack and strapped it across her chest, and slung the tarp sack of food over her shoulder. Then she crouched down and summoned every ounce of motherly kindness left within her, which seemed unnatural even after all these years. Gods, she'd never wanted to be a mother, and never would've been if not for her love of Peter, even as the world fell apart around them. But she was lucky that she still had Brynn after Peter was gone, if only for a time.

"You know, I just realized," Katla said in her best mom voice, "that I never asked your name."

"Tommy, ma'am," he said, looking at her in surprise. "What's yours, if you don't mind?"

"You can call me Kat," she replied. "I've got to be on my way, though. Will you walk with me, Tommy?"

"Of course, ma—I mean, Kat. But I can only go as far as the property line."

Katla nodded. Ghosts were tethered to their remains. "Then walk me as far as that, and then we'll say our goodbyes, okay, Tommy?"

Tommy nodded and gave her his winning, missing-toothed smile. "Okay, Kat."

A short time later, with the barn and the oak and the farmhouse far in the distance, Tommy stopped at a gravel road and said, "This is as far as I can go."

Katla stopped beside him and lowered herself into a crouch once more. "Tommy, thank you for everything. I'm so glad I met you." She propped her elbow on her knee and offered him her hand.

"I'm glad to have met you, too. But I'll just pass right through you, you know."

"Try me."

The ghost-child looked uncertain, but his small hand crept toward her outstretched palm. As their skin touched and her fingers closed around his, his form began to glow, and his grin spread wide.

"Thank you," he whispered just before he disappeared.

And Katla stood, hand still outstretched for a moment or two before it dropped to her side as she inhaled sharply, shakily, drawing back a sob.

"I hope you get where you're going, kid," she whispered to the empty air.

Katla Brynjólfsdóttir, deliverer of lost souls, said a derisive voice from behind her. Did you ever dream that this would be your life, back when you were doing taxes for a living?

"None of this is even real," Katla said under her breath, staring at her palm where she'd touched the boy. She didn't have to see the one-eyed dog to know that it was watching her from the overgrown cornfield. "The world ended and I have magic powers. It's preposterous."

That's not what your witch of a mother would have said.

"My mother was a woman of science. She was no witch."

You speak of her as if she were dead. As if she hadn't sent your daughter to summon you to her.

"Oh, what do you know?" Katla snapped. The bigger question on her mind was how he knew it, but she wouldn't give him the satisfaction of asking.

Oh, please. The dog rolled its one good eye. *Humans have been trying to reconcile science and faith since before you were even a thought. You think your parents were any different?*

He does have a point, child. The sparrow landed on a post in front of her. *Civilization as you know it has ceased to exist. Is it so hard to believe that a little magic is creeping its way back into the world?*

"You're wrong. My parents did what they could to help, and I can guarantee you it didn't involve magic." She spat the word as if it were as foul as the Plague itself.

How can you be sure about that? asked the dog. *They both followed the old gods.*

Katla cast a menacing glance at the sky and thought of Space Station Earth, thought of that drawing in her picture book, of the remains of Asgard.

"Then the old gods were useless, too," she said, and set off down the gravel road toward Gimli.

***

She hiked through the rest of Nebraska and the Dakotas, resting where she could and trying to keep up her strength, for she had started feeling a bit weak even with her extra provisions. She'd been walking parallel to the interstates her entire trip; she wished for a forest, for the cover of trees, but the plains never seemed to end.

The Plague fully came upon her a few miles into Canada. She knew she must've caught it from the boy's corpse. The symptoms sometimes took weeks to manifest.

But she did not stop.

She shivered with fever despite the heat. Her limbs felt like they weighed a thousand pounds and it was a struggle to put one foot in front of the other. There were times when her progress slowed to a literal crawl, when she took shelter in empty houses—against her vow to avoid them, and the ghosts within—because she was too weak to pitch her tent.

The road signs said she was skirting Winnipeg proper. Closer. Getting closer.

"I did not come all this way," she huffed as she dragged herself along, her cold skin slick with sweat, "to die by the side of the road in the middle of nowhere."

That's the spirit, kid, said the one-eyed dog, trotting along beside her.

It occurred to her, then, that the dog and the sparrow had been speaking to her in Icelandic this entire time—Icelandic, but not quite—and her brain had understood.

"Maybe we'll find a sled and you can make yourself useful and drag me to Gimli," she said, and thought the dog replied that it was against the rules, but Katla didn't have the strength to ask.

***

It was getting dark.

Relief settled over her when she caught sight of the sign marking the city limits, and she veered west into the woods. She was so close. She knew the forest well, having explored it as a preteen and teenager. She'd wanted to take Brynn to see her grandmother and play here, but they never managed the trip, not with Brynn being born right at the beginning of the Collapse. Not with the threat of war, and the Plague...

Voices up ahead, lights in the clearing where she knew her mother's cabin to be. Her vision blurred, her steps faltered. She pitched herself forward and began to crawl, her glasses askew from the fall. She couldn't so much as make a sound.

The lights danced in front of her eyes, and the din of voices grew louder. Who's there? It sounded like so many people. Too many people. She could make them out, but in the moonlight she couldn't tell if the figures were ghosts or living, breathing humans.

Finally the last of her strength gave out and she rolled onto her back, staring up at the moon shining down between the tree branches.

Just a moment. I'll just rest a moment. I'm almost there.

The next time she opened her eyes, she couldn't move her body, and her mother was kneeling above her, gray hair a halo around her head, the outline of her body silver in the moonlight. Is she a ghost?

Katla was in the clearing now. There were more faces beyond her mother's, within her line of vision. And a cabin just beyond them, the clearing full of tents.

Am I dead? Katla felt someone take her hand and knew it was her mother. She wanted to scream at them not to touch her because she had the Plague, or not to touch her or they would disappear—her mother's skin was cold just like the ghost-child's had been, and she couldn't exorcise her own mother, not after losing Brynn—but she couldn't speak.

"My brave daughter," said that warm voice from her childhood, just before the people around her flickered and glowed and everything faded to black. "It's finally time to rest."

***

The one-eyed dog and the sparrow looked on from beyond the clearing. If anyone had noticed them at that exact moment and seen them from just the right angle, they might not have seen two creatures but a man in a broad-brimmed hat and tattered traveling cloak, using a spear as a walking stick, and a woman in a rich red mantle with a feathered cape draped over one arm and a golden necklace gleaming at her collar.

"It doesn't count if she dies," the man grunted to his companion.

"She won't," the woman said serenely. "Her mother has the cure."

A beat passed as the man stared at her. "You knew this when you chose her, didn't you? That her parents followed the old path. That her mother came up with—"

"Fair's fair." The woman's expression betrayed nothing. "She made it here, and I chose her. That's a point for me, and now I'm in the lead."

"Hmm." He shifted, grumping. "The girl has magic in her. You're a cheater."

"It takes one to know one."

He had nothing to say to that besides, "Well, on to choose the next foundling. We have many more lost souls to guide. Let's make haste," and he turned to leave.

"Of course," replied the woman with a catlike grin as she followed him into the darkness. "This new world won't build itself, after all."

Sweet Little Lies

Lindsey Duncan

Lindsey Duncan is a chef / pastry chef (CPC CSW), professional Celtic harp performer and life-long writer, with short fiction and poetry in numerous speculative fiction publications. Her contemporary fantasy novel, Flow, is available from Double Dragon Publishing, and her science fiction novel, Scylla and Charybdis, is out from Grimbold Books. She feels that music and language are inextricably linked. She lives in Cincinnati, Ohio and can be found on the web at http://www.LindseyDuncan.com

Ilanor struggled upright in her bed as cold hands grabbed her shoulders and feet. She opened her mouth to shout, more angry than frightened, but shadows shifted and flowed down her throat, silencing her protests. Instinctively, she gasped for breath even as she recognized the effect as illusion.

No one would come to her rescue. It was the night after Lady Cirowyn's betrothal feast, a twelve-course cacophony of dishes from every known realm, and Ilanor had been the only one still awake in the dorms. The others snored around her.

The shrouded figures carried her like a corpse. She tried to get enough leverage to kick. What would an illusionist want with her? The imperial court ruled the inner city, but the outer city— where Ilanor lived—was the domain of entertainers and known as the City of Veils. She shouldn't rate a second glance, even as assistant to one of the most infamous chefs in the Imperial Capital.

Her captors deposited her in a chair in her employer's parlor. Portraits stared down in disapproval as she scrambled into a more dignified position.

The fireplace burst into flames, dancing greens and purples amongst more traditional hues. The flames did not fully illuminate the figure leaning against the mantle.

Spidery white hands, delicate as paper, lay on the stone. "My people tell me your name is Ilanor."

"What do you want?" she asked, veins singing with tension.

"What does anyone want? Fame and fortune, a place in history..." He waved it off. "You have a talent for illusion."

Ilanor shook her head. "I'm a baker. My talents are for water, flour, sugar, and eggs." Though aching and repetitive, there was nothing like the tactile pleasure of dough in her hands.

"Allow me the arrogance of understanding my work, mistress Ilanor," he said. "Suffice to say, I require your services as an apprentice. I'll increase what you're being paid by five opal marks a week, and of course when your term is done, all the finer opportunities in life await."

The sum made her dizzy. "I'll pass."

He gestured to his companions. One clamped down on Ilanor's shoulder; the other knelt and pressed something to her ankle. She heard a latch click. She shoved them away, leaning down to probe it with her fingers. It burned as if hot out of the oven. She cried out.

"That wasn't a question." He sounded apologetic. "What you're wearing now is an Imbrizi band. I have the other in my pocket. When I wear it, I can monitor your location. If I don't like what I sense, the bracelet will force you to remain where you stand, your feet like stone."

She stared, unable to make sense of the words. "You're going to force me? Why not just pick from the hopefuls that swarm the city?"

"How many of them do you really think have the aptitude? I

have my reasons. As I've already paid off your master, no one will miss you."

That smarted, more than being cornered. "I'm good at what I do."

A faint smile. "I'm sure. In time, you'll thank me." He peered into the flames; they flicked into nothingness. "Come with me."

Even without the illusion that obscured her sight, Ilanor would never have been able to retrace the turns they took. They entered a manor house in the innermost City of Veils with walls filigreed like lace. A guard guided her to an immense bedchamber appointed with a bed big enough to drown in.

"This is your room," the illusionist said. "You have free run of this part of the house, but you are not to go downstairs into the servant quarters. Do you understand?"

Because he was hiding her, she realized. "What am I going to put in that dresser, uniforms for an army?"

"Appropriate attire will be provided," he said.

Ilanor thought about the frilly robes and elaborate hairpieces illusionists wore. "If I see a corset, I'm going to string you up with the laces."

"I suggest you rest." He had the audacity to smile before he stepped out.

Trying to hide the quiver in her knees, Ilanor stalked to the rug and curled up. She was not sleeping in that monstrosity of a bed; she would never find her way out again.

***

The guard shook her awake. He thrust a cup of too-sweet

firejuice at her. He ignored her attempts at conversation. Once she set the cup aside, he pushed her up interminable staircases into a richly-appointed tower chamber. It shone like a festival.

Under the gleam of conjured lights, she could finally see the illusionist clearly. He was younger than she had expected, with no more than two decades on her nineteen years. His auburn curls were shorn close at the neck, yet hung over his brow.

It took her a second to recognize him in the plain white robe, but the mismatched eyes—one brown, one green—of High Illusionist Tanniv Deronas were unmistakable. As the chosen conjurer of the Cirowyn line, he occupied one of the most prominent places in outer-city society. Once the Cirowyns achieved control over another kingdom, which would happen with their daughter's wedding, they would be next to the emperor himself.

"Your patrons have a feast to end all feasts, and you spend your time poking around in the kitchens?" she demanded.

He regarded her mildly. "With that much mead, no one needs an illusionist. Can we begin?"

What choice did she have? "Are you still going to pay me?"

"Seems only fair." Tanniv spread his hands. The gesture revealed where he wore the other bracelet, high on his right arm. She narrowed her eyes.

At his gesture, the guard slipped out. "Illusion involves manipulating the underlying forces of the universe to create misleading phenomena. Fooling the eyes is the simplest part and involves bending rays of light. You must understand," his voice sharpened, "that attention to detail is critical. Every step must be executed to perfection and every sense invoked."

"I know how to do that," she said, fighting her temper. Of course he didn't understand or respect a baker's craft.

Tanniv eyed her. "We're not rattling amongst pots and pans now, my dear. This is delicate work."

"Clearly," she countered, "you've never tried to prepare a red velvet cake with boiled buttercream frosting."

"I should think that would be obvious. The problem with food is no one notices it unless it is bad," Tanniv said. "Illusion, on the other hand, commands attention, and just as the flaws become more glaring, the successes are more crucial."

Ilanor bit her tongue. What had she expected from a man who had no worries but aesthetic pleasure and simpering at his employers?

"To create an illusion of a specific sense, you first heighten your awareness of that sense. A raw student such as yourself can learn this focus by stating the name of every color you see in your surroundings." He waited, brows arched, clearly expecting to have to coach her.

She flitted a look around her. "Gray. White. Red." She continued to scan. "Gold, mint, saffron, cinnamon, iron, scarlet, beet..." Everything came into sharp focus. She noticed the knots and snagged threads in the curtains, the roughened flecks in the stone, and every contour and dot of pigment in his face.

With it came a peculiar sensation: a knowledge behind the sight, like tasting a pastry and knowing how it had been made. She could sense where light absorbed and where it reflected, and the web made by imperceptible flows of warmth and energy. Despite herself, her lips parted with a sharp intake of breath.

"It's remarkable, isn't it?" Tanniv's voice was warm, sharing the wonder. "If you move, do so slowly—the trance is easy to break."

Something more: a light inside herself, Ilanor realized, a mass of writhing incandescence. Was this the talent he had seen in her? Instinctively, she focused on Tanniv, trying to see his talent. Her eyes clouded with shadow, and she teared up.

"Enough," he barked. "Look away." She did, rubbing her eyes. "Standard practice for an illusionist of stature," he said brusquely. "Can't reveal to our competition how strong we are."

Or how weak, she resisted the urge to point out.

"I want you to fix on that inner light. Let it expand. It will become a second set of hands. A skilled illusionist can work with more than one sense at once—only the best—" did he have to say 'Such as himself?' Clearly, he thought not, "—can manage them all. Adding the various senses in layers is time-consuming, but I wouldn't expect anything more from you for a while."

Ilanor ignored the barb, focusing until the light flowed into her fingertips. "If it's so time-consuming," she said, "maybe you shouldn't babble on."

"Are you always this surly? Put your hand in the stream of light coming from the window and lower it. You'll feel a resistance. Push down."

Ilanor followed his directions. Invisible force gathered under her fingers like kneaded dough. It responded to her touch, both tough and pliant. A cord of shadow formed under the pressure. She caught her breath. There was something thrilling about it, this shape she had created from nothing.

"It's like food," she said. "You can't actually make something out of thin air. You have to work with the resources you have."

"If you'd like to think of it that way, yes." His tone was brisk. "We're going to borrow elements of color from the curtains..."

***

By the end of the first lesson, Ilanor had formed something with the color and vague appearance of a rose. Another frustrating session and a clever person might have been able to guess she had created a book. Part of her wanted to be excited, but progress seemed so slow.

One morning, she decided she couldn't do worse by experimenting on her own. She pulled red from the hint of dawn, brown from unswept dirt, and spun them together with dappling sheen. Her heart quickened with delight.

"That's more like it," Tanniv said from behind. "Not sure I agree with the choice of subject matter, but it will do."

She jumped, but managed to hold the apple steady. "You have to give me something I'm familiar with," she said. "I only read recipes, and my only experience with gardens is when I'm throwing out scraps."

He arched a brow. "We shall certainly have to fix that."

There were scores of public gardens in the outer city, and his guards dragged her to them until her head ached with perfume, though her soul sang with prismatic tones. Tanniv inundated her with books about fashion and art, and she labored through the elaborate texts with a vow of vengeance every time she stumbled over a three-syllable word. The lessons became easier: he conceded on the subject matter, allowing that food was suitable for a harvest scene, and her first experiment with sound was clattering pots.

"Dreadful din," he dismissed it, "but realistic enough. Just—for the life of me!—don't ever do it again."

She made sure to practice the tonal patterns whenever he passed by.

He demonstrated few techniques. When he did summon illusions himself, he seemed distractible: they were thin and almost transparent.

In other circumstances, she might have enjoyed her lessons. The concoction of illusion was as painstaking as a seven-layered torte. She found her touch growing surer without words to describe how.

Ilanor always had questions, the urge to dig deeper. In the kitchens of autocratic bakers, she had been silenced. Tanniv answered questions of theory with alacrity, though he sometimes went on far longer than she wanted. He roused her out of a nap one afternoon. "We need to start work now. I have a project for you—a serious project—will you up! Did you respond this slowly when rats got into the grain?"

"Rats never got into the grain," Ilanor mumbled, pulling the blanket over her head, "and that wasn't my job if they had."

"Well, I am paying you to deal with the metaphorical rats." He snapped his fingers. "Out."

She flung the blanket at him and sat up. "Fine. What do you want me to do?" "An ivory flute that plays of its own accord. For the front door of the new Cirowyn steward." He scrubbed at his face. "Blast, it was supposed to be another week and a half before he arrived."

"But I don't—"

"It will only need to play a few snatches of tune," he assured her, "and you seem to have a tolerable ear. I have no time for your self-doubts."

"I don't even know how many holes a flute has," she said.

"Do you ever pay attention to the finer points of things that don't immediately concern you?"

"Do you?" she countered.

He whirled away, ignoring the question. "The basic form first."

Ilanor followed his directions, correcting where he pointed out flaws. They squabbled over the choice of tune, neither with the advantage; she couldn't craft music without him, and he couldn't teach her to imbue a song she didn't know.

The finished flute was a thing of beauty, gold filigree weaving around the holes. Twenty-four notes played in an endless loop, pure like the whistling of steam and the rustling of morning birds, which Tanniv confessed he was rarely awake to hear. For the first time, she saw admiration in his eyes.

"Bend the rim into a loop," he instructed. "Tie it together—carefully! Break it free of the surrounding energy and—"

She cried out when he brought his hands down on the flute, compressing it into nothing. He arched a brow, then drew his hands apart. The flute materialized again. "How else did you think you moved them?"

"I was just worried you'd bust it with your clumsiness," she said, covering for her dismay.

Tanniv smiled slightly. "I'll send my dresser in with your robes."

He was halfway out the door when she caught up to him. "Wait— my robes?"

"Yes, is there a problem?"

"Why do I have robes?"

"You're coming with me," he said.

She swallowed, her stomach fluttering. "You didn't take my measurements."

"You're not a tricky fit. Thick waist, narrow hips, and long neck. The numbers are not difficult to estimate."

Her voice rose in indignation. "You've been staring at me?"

"Yes, and I found it something of a trial." He sighed. "Could you be quiet the two seconds required to dress?"

She kicked the door after him, muttering curses. His dresser, a stout, florid woman, yanked her headfirst into a lavender robe with a scalloped neck. Even with the sash around her waist, she felt undressed. The woman batted her hands away long enough to force a brush through her hair.

The dresser turned her to the mirror. She confronted a sculpted version of herself, as if an illusionist had decided to play a trick on the world. The fabric swished sensuous across her skin, and for a heartbeat she felt almost fine enough for the gilded role.

The door flew open. Tanniv stood there in some impossible

flourish of gold and emerald and looking as if he would combust at a touch. "Are you—"

"You don't burst into a woman's chamber!" Ilanor whirled, snatching up her tunic from her bed and holding it before her like a shield.

He regarded her with a frown, tensed to deliver a retort, then laughed. The next words sounded approving. "Put ten of you on the war-front and foreign armies wouldn't have a chance. Come on, and don't speak unless someone shoves a hot poker between your lips."

"Is anyone actually likely—" she started. He held up a hand to silence her.

They headed to the stables. The driver helped them into the carriage. She strained out the window as they moved, trying to identify streets, but Tanniv kept interrupting her with a finger snap and impatient directions as to precisely how to stand, how to hold her hands, and distinctly how not to respond to the noble pair.

Ilanor had seen the inner city and its mad flush of splendor before, but never entered its manors by front gates, much less with the reverent courtesy of everyone they passed. The Cirowyn great hall would fit her former employer's residence twice over. While she tried to read the illuminated lettering on the tapestries, Tanniv pulled her down a hallway.

A spidery servant stood sentinel. He bobbed his head and opened the door. "Their excellencies gave instructions that you were to be let in immediately."

The private sitting chamber reminded her of a jeweled box, with Lord Keltan and Lady Hilre merely the two largest stones within the settings. Tanniv swung into an elaborate bow; Ilanor dropped as low as she could without falling over, locked her leg muscles, and hoped she could hold onto the position.

"Tanniv!" Hilre stood in a swell of skirts. "So wonderful to see you. Whoever is this creature?"

"If it pleases your excellencies," Tanniv said, "my new apprentice, Ilanor."

"Since when do you take on apprentices, Tanniv?" Keltan rumbled, voice like a mountain avalanche. "You're not planning on retiring on us, are you?"

"Of course not." He sounded...nervous? Ilanor risked a peek. His neutral expression looked forced.

"Oh, let the poor dear relax," Hilre said. "She looks uncomfortable. Ilanor, would you care to sit down?"

Ilanor ignored Tanniv's glare and bobbed upright. "Thank you, your excellency, I'd like that." For the first time in her life, she got a direct look at a noblewoman's eyes—soft sky blue, but like anyone else's. She scuttled to the indicated chair. Velvet notwithstanding, it was hard and angled.

The trio conversed over her head, Hilre sweet and banal, Keltan vaguely discontent, and Tanniv respectful to the point of reverence. Ilanor had the suspicion he had expected similar treatment from her, that he had put her as far below him on the grand scale as the Cirowyns were above him. It explained a few things.

He showed them the illusory flute. Hilre cooed appreciatively.

"Suppose it will do," Keltan said. "You keep a good standard, Tanniv."

Ilanor shifted on the chair. Tanniv silenced her with a look.

"Thank you, your excellency. I'm glad such poor workings please you."

She stifled a spurt of indignation. That was her work he was maligning! But it seemed to be the game, to abase himself with a knowing smile. She shouldn't care. She was doing this because she had no choice, and the money would be useful when it was over. She could rent rooms, get out of the dormitories, take steps towards a kitchen of her own.

Tanniv instructed the Cirowyns on how to place the illusion, asked them to pass his greetings on to their daughter, and ushered Ilanor out.

A stunning blonde woman descended from a carriage. Ilanor recognized the silver silk that pooled around her: the robe of a senior illusionist. Tanniv stiffened, clutching Ilanor's shoulder.

"Tanniv! So good to see you," the woman said. "You've been absent so long, we feared you were ill." She regarded him through lowered lashes. "You're not ill, are you?"

"I've been busy, Betra," he said.

Her hands lilted in a summoning gesture. "With...?"

"My apprentice, for one." He pushed her forward like a sacrificial offering. "Ilanor, this is High Illusionist Betra Sindasri. Betra, this is Ilanor."

Betra's brows rose, the question obvious in her eyes: Ilanor who? Only common folk had no surname. "Charmed, I'm sure. How soon do you expect to replace him, Ilanor?"

Ilanor's first impulse was to run with the jest, but something about the woman made her uneasy. "Probably never," she said. "Figure a man like him doesn't need replacing."

Betra laughed. "Oh, I'm sure he'll go crusty and his powers will wither eventually. Don't be a stranger, Tanniv! Good to meet you, Ilanor." She tossed him a last look and sailed up the drive.

"Who was—"

"In the carriage," he said shortly. "Now." Only when the inner city fell behind did he speak again. "Betra is the personal illusionist of Lord Harmac, Elen Cirowyn's betrothed. She and I have been at odds for years. With the betrothal and Lord Harmac being of lesser stature, he becomes a Cirowyn and—you see where I'm going with this, yes?"

"Sort of," Ilanor said.

"There are a number of unpalatable possibilities, from one of us being fired to the other being designated as a junior." Tanniv grimaced. "Better a junior in the Cirowyn household than the senior illusionist anywhere else, but Betra won't rest until she's ruined me."

"Why?"

"It's the way things are done, and she'd expect the same from me. There was a time she would have been right, but...I'm tired of it, I suppose."

Ilanor almost felt sorry for him—or would have, without the silks and splendor. "And you wonder why I just want to bake," she said.

"As it happens," he responded drily, "I still do."

She rolled her eyes. There was no arguing with the man.

***

The next weeks became routine. Tanniv had Ilanor craft three more illusions for the Cirowyns, each of increasing complexity. Trapped in Tanniv's estate, following his directives, helping him with a political game she didn't understand...it made her bones itch. Their exchanges of quips took the edge off. She had the sneaking suspicion he enjoyed it.

One day, they worked on smells in the garden. He shaped an example for her, perfume. She inhaled, found it cloying but inoffensive. She turned her thoughts on him, caught a whiff of the smoke barrier that surrounded him, and drew it into her lungs despite his shouting.

He grabbed her shoulders and shook her. Her nose cleared, but not before she got a whiff of what was behind the barrier.

"Something's wrong with you," she said.

"I'm not the one who just—" to his credit, Tanniv stopped, with a guilty look down at the anklet she wore. "What's going on with me is not your business."

"You made it my business when you paraded me in public," she said. "I'm your apprentice. Anyone who thinks they can get at you because of...whatever this is might decide to come through me."

He turned away. "No one knows what is going on, and it will stay that way."

"Your powers are damaged," she said. "They're not working the way they should. Am I right?"

"I begin to think you're more trouble than you're worth." He couldn't muster any heat in his voice. "If I tell you, will you leave off?"

"Depends on what I hear."

Tanniv barked laughter. "I think I find that more reassuring than an empty promise. Sit." He eased himself onto a stone bench, weariness dripping into his frame. "The skill never dies. Decades of finesse, experience, contemplation—these things are the mark of an exceptional illusionist, and can never be erased.

"The talent, on the other hand...I'm dry. Have been since three months before I recruited you." He had the grace to stumble over the word. "I don't know what happened. If there were warning signs, I didn't notice. I don't think it was sabotage, but the force that brings illusion together—gone."

Ilanor was surprised by the stirrings of sympathy. He had thrown his life into it, staked his world on his abilities, and there were no explanations, no one to blame.

"I'm so sorry," she said.

He looked away and said nothing. They sat in indecisive silence. Now she understood the melodramatic abduction, the Imbrizi band, though she could not entirely forgive him for it. Indignation swirled on her tongue: if he had simply asked...but he didn't live in a world where people could be trusted.

"I'm not staying forever," she said. "If this is what your job puts you through, I don't want it. But I will stay."

He chuckled weakly. "I am an unusual case. I've never heard of this happening."

"That doesn't mean anything. They could have done exactly what you're doing," she said. "Why me?"

"The hopefuls who stream into the city every year are the children of minor nobles and rich merchants—people who have enough money to foot the bill while they wait for an illusionist to be interested in them." Tanniv snorted. "They're owned, marked, somebody's puppet.

"Besides," he continued, "you do have a remarkable amount of potential. It's a shame to waste it on stews."

"Actually, my specialty is cakes," she said.

He rubbed his face. "Bear with me until after the wedding? Whatever's going to happen will fall out before then."

Three months. It was longer than she wanted, but it was the first time there had been an end to it—and the first time he had asked. "Deal," she said.

He pushed himself up. "Well. Shall we back to work?"

"Let's." Truce, she thought, reciting the list of scents.

***

The wedding drew nearer. Despite newfound patience in their lessons, Tanniv looked older and moved like it.

One day, head throbbing, she abandoned practice and prowled in a direction forbidden to her. She needed to clear her head, and the only way to do that was to get her hands dirty.

She slipped down to the kitchen. When not wearing apprentice robes, she could have been anyone. A cook thumped out the dough for a cherry morning cake.

Ilanor slid in next to her. "Mind if I help?"

The woman pushed the bowl of fruit over. "Wash those."

She came back with the cherries to find the cook fighting with frosting that had turned to sludge. "Here," she said, "you don't want to add any more sugar or it will harden too much."

No one asked why Ilanor was there, and she fell into the routine. She chatted with the women, sharing tips and coated to her elbows in flour. She was stunned how comfortable it was. She hadn't realized how much of a strain her apprenticeship put on her.

She convinced the head cook to purchase ingredients for an exotic northshore ice-cake she knew would be a delicacy even for Tanniv. It was a recipe she had never prepared and longed to, and she might give him the idea there was some art to it.

"What is going on here?"

She hadn't even heard footsteps before Tanniv thundered into the kitchen. She jerked around, swinging in front of the worktable to shield its contents.

"You," he snapped. "Out. Now."

"I'm taking a break," she said. "Mind your own business."

"We have an arrangement." His voice was crisp and hard. "Splashing about like a child playing in mud puddles was not part of it."

"Don't worry, I'm not going to mess up your imaginary friends," she bit back. "I know they're the only ones you have."

He caught her arm, jerking her back. She jammed her elbow into his ribs. His hand came about with a sharp crack against her cheek.

She stood motionless, shaking. He stared, eyes wide, as stunned as she was. "Get out," he said, this time to the staff. They fled.

Ilanor tried not to tremble. "I just needed…"

"You're better than this kind of menial work," he said, "or if you're not, now is the time to pretend."

"It's not menial, it's an art—my art."

"And our survival doesn't depend on that art." Tanniv sucked in a breath, looking as if he would shatter. "Clean up. I don't want to see you here again."

Ilanor's body clenched. If he wanted his work, he would have it, but their understanding was finished.

***

They didn't speak of the argument. The lessons become cold, formal, no unnecessary words exchanged. One week later, Ilanor lay curled on the rug when a knock came.

It was his dresser with a fancier variant on her formal robes. "Master says you're coming with him to an event tonight."

"Can you tell him he can walk off a cliff?" Ilanor said.

The dresser sighed. With the extensive wardrobe of even an apprentice, they had spent a fair amount of time together—and by simple necessity, she was the only other person who knew about the Imbrizi band. They had developed a certain understanding. At least, she knew not to be shocked by Ilanor's temper. "I get in trouble if you're difficult, miss. Would you please?"

Ilanor submitted, stewing, but on her way to the stables, she considered. There would be plenty of people at a party, those who would wonder and perhaps ask questions. If she could get Tanniv in trouble without revealing his disability, she might have a chance to escape.

No word passed between she and Tanniv until they arrived at the home of a minor noble. He held her arm and murmured, "Remember everything you say reflects on me...and like a doubled mirror, it comes back to you."

She hadn't intended to, but the anxiety in his voice softened her response. "I understand."

The music was familiar, though she had never been so surrounded by its ebbs and flows. Impossible color swirled past her, gowns and cravats and elaborate feathered hats. Who needed illusion when reality was so vivid?

By habit, she found herself picking out detail, noticing the reflection of jewels and the shadows cast by petticoats. The press of people overwhelmed her, and she squirmed through the crowd into a garden capped with lanterns like stars. She leaned against a stone pillar.

"Beautiful night, isn't it?" Betra's perfume preceded her.

Ilanor stiffened. Her instincts warned her about this woman, but Betra was Tanniv's enemy, not hers. "Hard to take it all in."

"One gets accustomed to these things before long." Betra's voice was one part reassurance, two parts inquiry.

Ilanor made herself shrug. "I don't like to let anything get commonplace."

"You sound like your mentor. We don't have to be enemies, you know. I would scarcely blame you for Tanniv's faults."

"Good. I'm not in this to make enemies." The anklet itched. Did he know where she was?

"What about friends?"

"I...maybe." She bunched her fingers in her robe. All she had to do was lift it a fraction.

"Here's some advice, as a friend." Betra smiled faintly. "Even if the sins of your mentor amount to treason, you can't be hanged with him—if you have protection."

What, if anything, did Betra know? Ilanor had never considered what the punishment for having an Imbrizi band was. She knew the reaction Betra expected—a combination of panic and ambition—but she found herself indignant instead. Betra thought of her as a commoner, a thing to be used and manipulated. Ilanor couldn't stomach that. At least Tanniv saw her talents for illusion and trusted her to honor her end of their bargain. She had made a deal with him; she would keep it.

"That's a low thing to say," Ilanor said, turning.

"Oh, don't let me drive you away," Betra said, stepping past her. They got tangled, and Ilanor stumbled. The illusionist supported her with an arm, a solicitous touch. "Enjoy your sanctuary, Ilanor."

She disappeared on a cloud of perfume, and Ilanor slumped against the pillar. She noticed, in the half-light, a long rip in the robe, and grimaced—but it didn't connect that it might be anything more than an inconvenience.

***

A flurry of knocking awoke Ilanor. She pulled herself up, grunting, and realized she was still dressed from the evening before. "Go away, Tanniv."

"Miss! Let me in."

It was the dresser. Ilanor scuffed to her feet, pulling the door open. The woman's face was red and puffy.

Ilanor squinted. "What's going on?"

"The emperor's men just took the master into custody," the dresser said. "Betra accused him of planning to use an Imbrizi band on Lady Elen."

"What?" Ilanor heard a soft click. Startled, her gaze jerked down as the anklet fell away. "Why did it release?"

"The guards must have removed the master band. There's no proving you were wearing it now, miss."

"Except my word." Ilanor might have been irritated with Tanniv, but she realized she had looked forward to her lessons, the next challenge. "What am I supposed to do?"

"You're free now."

"I know." Ilanor rubbed at her ankle. "I could just go home." Her life had been given back to her, but the price for treason was death. She had railed at him...but she could never wish him dead.

Her hands drifted, finding the tear in the robe. She swore.

"Miss?"

"I ripped my robe," she said, the truth burning off the haze of confusion. "Betra must have seen the band and thought she could get away with this. I have to go to the emperor. I have to explain—"

The dresser stopped her. "If you tried to approach the guard as his apprentice, they would arrest you for conspiracy."

In a way, wasn't that accurate? The conspiracy she had undertaken was hiding Tanniv's loss of power, and it had thrown her into a new world. She had told Tanniv that baking was her art, and she didn't want to leave it behind—but she wasn't ready to leave this world, either. She had too much to learn about illusion and its expression, the ephemeral touch of it under her hands.

She thought of her first lesson and how she had compared the power to bread dough. "Then I'm going in as a baker."

"That still won't get you near the emperor, miss."

Ilanor turned the anklet over, her mind supplying her with an image of Tanniv compressing the illusory flute: folded out of sight, to emerge whenever it was needed.

She knew, as if it had been whispered to her, exactly what to do.

"If the guard comes back," she said, "tell them Tanniv's apprentice is out of town with her sick mother." She headed to the kitchens. She pulled the sash off to tie up her hair; the sleeves got tucked up to her elbows.

"Did you order the ingredients for the ice-cake?" she asked.

The head cook blinked. "Aren't you—"

"Right now, I'm your best hope of this job still being here in three days," Ilanor said.

"Everything is in the storerooms now. What do you want to do?"

"What I'm best at," she replied. "We're making that cake."

It was a delicate, painstaking process, with a mistake at any juncture meaning they would have to dump the batter and start anew, and every layer had to be frozen before the next was added.

Ilanor and the cooking staff went through most of Tanniv's stored ice maintaining the required temperatures.

And one thing more: while the core chilled, Ilanor crafted the illusion. She needed sight, snatches of darkness; sound, the whispers of voices remembered; and a touch of fear she didn't have to fake. The only way to acquit Tanniv of one crime was to admit another. She recreated the scene.

"What you're wearing now is an Imbrizi band..."

"You're going to force me?"

"I have my reasons..."

Finally satisfied—it wasn't technically perfect, but it was her best without days to review—she folded the illusion up. She eased it into the batter, where it melted like butter.

The results were fantastic: a dark raspberry liqueur in the center of a ring of shaved ice, with the marbled raspberry and cinnamon cake protecting both. Ilanor let out a long breath.

"Thank you," she said. "Now to the palace."

"I have a cousin who works there, miss," said the head cook. "Do you want me to introduce you?"

***

Ilanor had never dreamed of entering the imperial palace, even through the kitchen doors. The emperor kept a massive staff; it was simple to put one more delicacy on the dessert tray. As soon as the cake was whisked out of sight, Ilanor resorted to fretting. She knew the emperor ate before his guests, but the food-taster was between him and the illusion.

Despite her worries, the kitchen routine soothed her. She watched the bustle of what was probably an ordinary meal, but looked like a holiday feast. More food than ten people could eat in a week went by with every dish.

Two palace guards navigated the kitchen. Her heart clenched when they approached her.

"Are you Ilanor?"

"Sometimes," she replied. "What's going on?" "The emperor wants to see you."

Good news? Bad? Was putting an illusion in the emperor's food considered poisoning him? What she said was: "It's about time."

The walls of the dining room were paneled with gold, the table inlaid with diamond, and the messy dishevel of a mostly finished meal lay in heaps and mounds. The cake, half-eaten, its core gelled out on the plate, sat before a pudgy individual overwhelmed by his robes of state.

The emperor.

Ilanor stared, trying to look past the splendor and seeing not much there. "How did you do this?" he asked, gesturing to the cake.

"It requires patience and access to enough ice to deep-freeze the inner layers," she answered, "but isn't terribly—"

One of the guards shoved her. She squawked and started to turn on him, but a low chuckle from the emperor interrupted her. "That wasn't what I meant. How did you insert the illusion inside it?"

She blinked. "I just did. It seemed to work."

"Your mentor came up with this idea, did he?" he said. "It's an intriguing concept, I have to say."

Didn't he understand what she had shown him? Ilanor fought a flare of aggravation. "No. It was mine. I didn't do this to amuse anyone." "You succeeded, even so," the emperor said. "Tell me more."

"It's a true story," she said, knowing it wasn't what he meant. "Tanniv never meant to use the band on Lady Cirowyn. He's not guilty of treason."

A long pause. The emperor sighed, as if it was a petty distraction. "By your own admission, he's guilty of holding you against your will. Why not leave him to the greater crime?"

"Because he doesn't deserve to die." Ilanor met his eyes. "All Tanniv Deronas ever tried to do is survive and practice his trade, and he does it like no one else. If there's one thing in all the world I understand—" she waved at the cake "—it's wanting to do what you love." "I see." The irritation faded, his expression becoming thoughtful. He turned to the guards. "Bring Tanniv to me."

Ilanor waited, staring down the ruler of the known realms across a cluttered table. The guards returned with Tanniv, his eyes reddened and his wrists chained together.

He stumbled to a halt. "Ilanor?"

The anxiety in his voice was unmistakable. She wanted to smile in reassurance, but she had no idea what the emperor was thinking.

"If this is you playing politics," she said instead, "you're terrible at it."

Tanniv chuckled. "I'm not sure you are the best mentor in that regard." He managed a stilted bow, hindered by the chains. "Your servant."

"This young woman informs me you held her with an Imbrizi band," the emperor said.

Tanniv winced. "The circumstances were—"

"I'm going to leave it to her to make a formal accusation," the emperor cut him off. "I have no interest in the interactions of peasants."

Ilanor flicked Tanniv a covert look, surprised the words hadn't summoned an indignant squawk.

"If the band was worn by this woman," the emperor continued, "it was never on the Lady Elen."

"It was never," Tanniv said fervently, "on the Lady Elen. She is my shining star."

Once again, the emperor simply trundled over the interjection. "If there is conspiracy here, it seems to be at the hands of the illusionist who brought the charges."

"Betra and I have long been at odds. She would do anything to—"

The emperor halted him with a lifted hand. "There will be a more thorough investigation, but until then, I release you." He gestured to the guards, who removed the shackles.

Tanniv wobbled. "If there is anything I can do—"

"There is. Your apprentice here seems to have found a unique use for your illusions. When placed inside a baked concoction, they materialize in the mind in extraordinary fashion." The emperor looked directly at Tanniv for the first time. "I wish to place you both on retainer to study this further."

Baking, with illusion, under the patronage of the emperor? Seeing her mentor too stricken to reply, Ilanor took it upon herself to be the voice of the obvious. "We'd love to."

"Then this audience is over. My steward will bring over the formal documents. I look forward to the results."

"I—thank you, your imperial highness," Tanniv stammered. Once outside the chamber, he turned to her. "You realize this doesn't mean I admit that your art is in any way on parallel with mine."

"That's a strange way of saying thank you," Ilanor said, "but since I rescued you, it seems only fair to stick around long enough to finish the job."

"I wonder how anyone found out about the band in the first—" He stopped, looking at her keenly. Perhaps he even thought she had done it on purpose. She flushed and started to speak, but he shook his head. "It doesn't matter. If we're going to do this, I insist upon perfect accuracy in your technique..."

"There's nothing wrong with my cake preparation," Ilanor interjected.

He arched a brow. "I thought we had agreed..."

They dickered down the corridor, neither one winning, neither one giving ground. Ilanor resisted a grin as they strode along, teacher and student—and it was no longer clear which was which.

THANK YOU TO OUR SUPPORTERS

Many thanks to our patrons and supporters, especially:

Anna O'Brien • Cathrin Hagey
Natalie Weizenbaum • S Naomi Scott
Johanna Levene • Stephanie Johnston

Aidan Long • BethOfAus • Bonnie Warford
carol shoemake • D.M. Domosea • Erik DeBill • Felicia
OSullivan • J'nae Spano • Katie Conrad • Kennon Hulett
Martin Cohen • Salomao Becker • Shannon White
Tamara Rutledge • Tory Hoke • Wanda • Frederick Stark

Ally Shaw • Brit Hvide • Carly Racklin • Charlotte Nash-Stewart
Dirck de Lint • Emily Anderson • GriffinFire • J. Askew
Jen G • Jocelyn Actual • Karen Anderson • Kayla • Kel
Kristina Saccone • Liz Warner • Maria Haskins • Rochelle B
Suzanne Thackston • Matthew Bennardo • Anne Worth

Want to see your name here? Become a patron!
patreon.com/lunastation

About the Cover Artist

Hello! My name is Serena Malyon and I'm a Canadian freelance illustrator. I grew up around art and spent my early days drawing medieval maidens and knights. In 2012 I graduated from the Alberta College of Art and Design, and I've built a career on my love of fantasy and adventure. I currently reside in Alberta with my boyfriend Nathan, where my hobbies include raising my 2 cats, playing RPGs and taking long walks in beautiful places.

You can find more of my work at:

http://serenamalyon.com

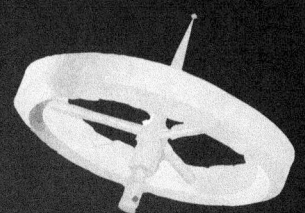

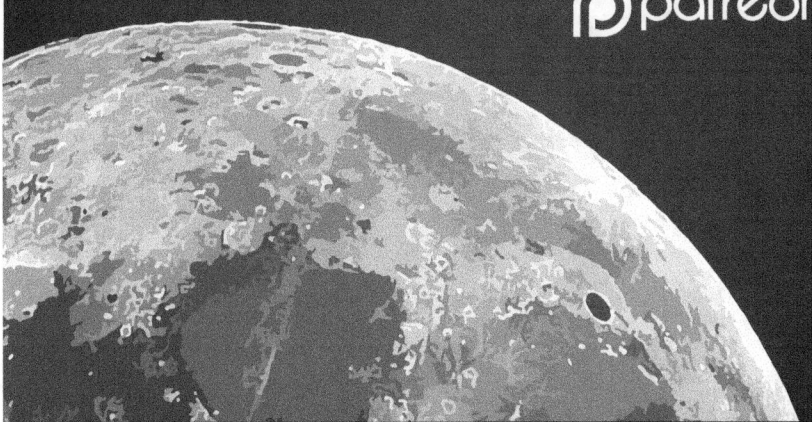